BALCO ATLANTICO

Also by Jérôme Ferrari in English Translation

Where I Left My Soul (2012)
The Sermon on the Fall of Rome (2014)

JÉRÔME FERRARI

BALCO ATLANTICO

Translated from the French by
David Homel

MACLEHOSE PRESS
QUERCUS · LONDON

First published in the French language as *Balco Atlantico* by
Editions Actes Sud, Arles in 2008
First published in Great Britain in 2019 by MacLehose Press

MacLehose Press
An imprint of Quercus Publishing Ltd
Carmelite House
50 Victoria Embankment
London EC4Y 0DZ

An Hachette UK company

A CIP catalogue record for this book is available
from the British Library.

ISBN (TPB) 978 0 85705 993 2
ISBN (Ebook) 978 1 84866 883 6

10 9 8 7 6 5 4 3 2 1

Designed and typeset in Albertina by Libanus Press Ltd
Printed and bound in Denmark by Nørhaven

Contents

for Tarik
for Jean

and for Norah

Oh my warriors, whither would you flee? Behind you is the sea, before you, the enemy. You have left now only the hope of your courage and your constancy. Remember that in this country you are more unfortunate than the orphan seated at the table of the avaricious master. Your enemy is before you, protected by an innumerable army; he has men in abundance, but you, as your only aid, have your own swords, and, as your only chance for life, such chance as you can snatch from the hands of your enemy. If the absolute want to which you are reduced is prolonged ever so little, if you delay to seize immediate success, your good fortune will vanish, and your enemies, whom your very presence has filled with fear, will take courage. Put far from you the disgrace from which you flee in dreams, and attack this monarch who has left his strongly fortified city to meet you. Here is a splendid opportunity to defeat him, if you will consent to expose yourselves freely to death. Do not believe that I desire to incite you to face dangers which I shall refuse to share with you. In the attack I myself will be in the fore, where the chance of life is always least.

The Commander of True Believers, Alwalid, son of Abdalmelik, has chosen you for this attack from among all his Arab warriors; and he promises that you shall become his comrades and shall hold the rank of kings in this country. Such is his confidence in your intrepidity. The one fruit which he desires to obtain from your bravery is that the word of God shall be exalted in this country, and that the true religion shall be established here.

From the speech of Tariq ibn Ziyad to his army
off the coast of Andalusia, 711.

MEMORY OVERLOAD

(October 2000)

Oh, Mama, Mama, I'm going to die, Virginie said, and her sobs were agonising, she felt like tiny stilettos were lacerating her lungs, oh, I will die, Mama, and Marie-Angèle, who loved her daughter more fiercely than all the hatreds she had felt in her life, tightened her embrace, turning her eyes away from the white sock splattered with mud and blood, and answered, yes, you will die of love, I know, and Virginie sobbed with gratitude and said it again, Mama, my life is over, and Marie-Angèle agreed, yes, my love, your life is over, over, and Virginie insisted, I loved him so much, Mama, I loved him so much, and Marie-Angèle told her, yes, you loved him, darling, and you'll always love him, you will never forget, don't worry, you will never forget.

No-one wants to hear that one day they will be cured of such pain. The idea of consolation can be intolerable, as Marie-Angèle knew well. She held her daughter close, and held her nose too, as if the horrible stink of shit that rose off the corpse in long, even, sugary waves had followed them into the house, and she knew that in a few months Virginie would recover her lust for life, though it was impossible to tell her that now. Oh, it will kill you, my love, Marie-Angèle whispered, you can be sure of it. Then she gave her something to make her sleep, took off her sock with a frown of disgust, and put her to bed. As I waited in the living room for Virginie to fall asleep, I was mesmerised by her indefatigable voice, vibrant with love and charity, that kept telling her that love would kill her. All those things that leave no trace except in our memory – of those things I cannot speak. Yet I still hear that voice with the same clarity as if it were next to me.

I had, it seems, spent a good portion of the afternoon at the bar, alone with Hayet, who was washing glasses in silence, and Vincent Leandri, who did not take his eyes off her. As usual he told me about his life on the shores of the Indian Ocean. He knew I had travelled and that I was in a better position than anyone in the village to understand what he was telling me. Since I've got to know him, he's talked about it more and more. He skips over his career as a nationalist militant, which ended after the fratricide of 1995, about which he says nothing, preferring to return to the dreams of his youth. "You see, Théodore," he told me, "there was this zebu with an incredibly stupid look, eating a plastic bag, it was blue, I remember. I had dragged myself into a bar to get a coffee, with the world's worst hangover. There was this guy behind the counter, the owner, a Frenchman, he looked like he was a hundred. And there was a Maori woman hunkered down next to him, some girl he must have been fucking, she was whistling and scratching her ass. I'm telling you, he looked like he was a hundred. He had the same stupid look as the zebu, with yellow eyes. He was missing a few teeth. I won't even describe the ones he had left. He was completely pickled in low-grade rum, he stank of cirrhosis and death, and I said to myself, how old is he, really? Forty? And I said to myself, that's you fifteen years from now if you stay here, that's you. It was like looking in a mirror, understand? That shook me up good, I panicked and came back here. I saved my own life, funny, no? I was proud of myself, I had the feeling I had actually saved my skin. If I had known, I would have been better off dying back there, from cirrhosis or the clap or whatever. Anything." He went on talking and I stopped paying attention to what he was saying. Vincent is never very happy to be alive, but that day he was particularly bad, a broken man. I could see that what he had become was the fruit of his downfall, I know of what I speak, yet it was almost impossible to think that this feeble old guy, who could scarcely look beyond his shoe tops, had been a strong, respected man five years earlier. In his case, the decline was total. That was probably why I found him likeable. I left him to ruminate by himself and went back to my house about the time Virginie came into the bar. Early in the evening, on my way to Marie-Angèle's, I came across the gendarmes from Olmiccia in front of her house. They were looking for clues around Stéphane Campana's body.

An hour before, Marie-Angèle explained, he parked and was

stepping out of his car when he got his guts blown out by two shots from a hunting rifle. When she heard the sound, Virginie came running out of her room, where she had holed up earlier that afternoon, no doubt to prepare herself in such a scandalously lubricious manner that her mother felt nauseous when she tried to imagine the nature of the preparations and where, apparently, she was waiting, stark naked, in her socks, her pudenda shaved. Whatever the case, that was how she presented herself, with the addition of a black band around her neck, when she sprinted down the stairs, crossed the living room where Marie-Angèle, her ears stuffed with earplugs, was trying to concentrate on her book, then dashed into the street and threw herself on her lover's corpse. Fifteen minutes later, the gendarmes found her in that position, sprawled over the body, perverting the crime scene with her screams, tears and nudity while her mother looked on, praying. Virginie continued to howl when they asked her nicely to move aside, and when the gendarmes finally tried to lift her off by force, she scratched one of them in the face, elbowed the second in the groin, bit the third on his hand and redoubled her howling, so the captain of the brigade was reduced to ordering her to be dragged away by her feet, which was what was done while she clung to the man she loved, trying to dig her fingers into his wounds, lick his blood and paint her face with it. As she struggled, she lost a sock that fell in the dust. Then she suffered a convulsion and let herself be pulled along the ground without further resistance. Her mother's arms closed around her and pulled her into the house.

The captain was intrigued. In the current political situation, there was no obvious reason that would explain the murder of a nationalist leader. Five years ago, and five hundred metres from there, in front of the bar, Dominique Guerrini, less lucky than his friend Vincent Leandri, had been killed in similar circumstances. But that was during the war between the underground factions and that war was long since over. The captain hoped the murder was not the sign of renewed hostilities. The other unexplained factor was the extraordinary stink the corpse was giving off. A police official examined the dead man's shoes and discovered shit deeply ingrained in the grooves of the textured soles. I turned to go back to Marie-Angèle, and as I left, I heard hysterical laughter and the sound of retching.

Marie-Angèle hugged her daughter's naked body very close, it was stained with bloody earth, and she almost felt Virginie was a baby again, she told me later that night, if it weren't for that single sock like a window swinging hideously open onto a world of perversion she would have preferred to know nothing about. She was shivering with hatred. Besides me, no-one knew the prayers she uttered before the body were really expressions of thanks. "Oh, Théodore! I'm not much of a believer but I thanked God for letting me gaze upon the corpse of that pig with my own eyes!" she told me – you see, she told me everything. At that very moment, the widow of Stéphane Campana was learning that her husband had gone and gotten himself killed in front of another woman's house, and that his last words to her had been lies, but Marie-Angèle didn't think about that. When Virginie was asleep, she took my hand, sat me next to her, and put her head on my shoulder as if seeking rest. She needed rest from the nine years of hatred and silence, rest from the eyes of Stéphane Campana staring at her daughter's crotch as she sat cross-legged on the wall by the fountain one summer night when she was thirteen, dressed in little blue cotton shorts, no bigger than a handkerchief and gaping open, rest from her inability to stand up to Virginie who forced the man's presence on her under her own roof, rest from the endless evenings vainly blocking her ears to keep from hearing the noises that echoed down from her room, not the sounds of love and tenderness, but a savage, unnamable racket of bestial coupling, because Virginie was too lost in love to maintain even the strict minimum of propriety, rest most of all from the recurrent expression on her daughter's face, it exhausted her, an expression of gravity and complete seriousness, the gravity and serious concentration that children are capable of, the absolute delight when she looked at him or thought of him, her devotion, her implacable stubbornness, her utter refusal to consider anything beyond the devastating insanity of her passion, and then constantly, what was worse, her expression of pure innocence, of immaculate awareness, "for my daughter is a kind of saint," Marie-Angèle told me, "the way my mother was a saint, the same race and the same ilk, made for the same kind of martyrdom."

At the age of ten, and this I took the trouble to note down, Marie-Angèle's mother had at her disposal no more than a dozen words with which to express herself, and it became clear that she would not acquire one more. She was, to her credit, a particularly pretty and docile little girl. She was allowed to wander through the village and out into the countryside as she loved doing. But when she was fifteen, she became pregnant. Her parents undertook an indignant but fruitless search to discover who in the village could have been guilty of so great an abomination. A boy was born to her, but died of heart failure a few weeks later, to the intense relief of her grandfather who was in no hurry to raise a bastard along with a feeble-minded little thing. A few months later, the war having broken out and the Italians occupying the region, Marie-Angèle's mother became pregnant again. The reassuring hypothesis of rape seemed less and less probable in her parents' eyes, and they had to face the painful fact that their daughter's moral sense was even less developed than her intelligence. Since there was a good chance that the father was an Italian soldier, which was intolerable, an old-fashioned abortion was carried out, using a knitting needle. Miraculously, Marie-Angèle's mother survived the procedure, which earned the family the unpleasantness of a priestly visit in order to officially benefit, through the grace of a common confession, from divine mercy. At the news of the third pregnancy, old Susini nearly killed her. He beat her to his heart's content with a stick, but got no more out of her than submissive whimpering and a look as overflowing with terror as it was devoid of any sense of guilt. They tried keeping her inside. That proved impossible. She screamed, cried, pounded her head against the door to her room and nearly split her skull open, and finally they had to free her. "Anyway, she's already pregnant," her father said. "Nothing worse can happen to us, she won't get a second bun in the oven." Thanks to heaven and, no doubt, the damage caused by her abortion, she had a miscarriage. In 1943, during the Liberation, they had to lock her up again, despite her howling. The village was full of Senegalese infantry and Moroccan regiments, and if they had to accept the eventual appearance of a bastard, at least let the thing be white. In 1946, she was pregnant again. When Marie-Angèle came into the world, everyone hoped she would die quickly, but she clung to life the way she had clung to the walls of a uterus wounded by knitting needles. The whole household viewed her with contempt and treated her coldly, except for her mother, who showered her with kisses and caresses until she died from her fifth pregnancy, six years later, with another dead bastard stuck in her belly. Everyone was satisfied that this source of continual dishonour had finally run dry. But the family's life was not improved – first because Marie-Angèle, this incarnation of shame, was very much alive, and it could not have been easy living in a village in which all the male inhabitants could be legitimately suspected of having abused a simple-minded girl. For Marie-Angèle, any man of a certain age whom she came across in the village streets, however affable he was, could have been her father, in other words, the worst kind of monster, and even, as she pointed out to me, far beyond those streets. At the age of twenty, she went to live at the other end of Corsica, in Calvi, where the beginnings of the tourism industry offered her work. She was hired as a waitress in a cabaret in the fortified old town. Despite her unhealthy distrust of men, she ended up living with a supposedly Hungarian member of the Foreign Legion who spoke some version of French with a horribly cosmopolitan accent but who, despite his tattoos and bulging muscles, treated her like a queen. "But inside every man there lives a pig, for sure," she told me one day, with bitterness. After several years of life together, she felt the need to confide in her Légionnaire and admitted for the first time that she was an illegitimate child. She also told him what sort of life her mother had led because, deep down, she was convinced that every human being should view that life with respect and compassion, the way she did. The stateless soldier feigned comprehension, but that night, when they made love, Marie-Angèle noticed several unpleasant changes. She rose and poured herself a glass of water, then returned to sit on the edge of the bed where the Légionnaire was displaying his muscles and staring at the ceiling. She told him that the next time he whispered those obscenities in her ear hoping to excite her, or if he looked at her just once the way he had looked at her that night, she would wait till he fell asleep and cut off his cock along with whatever was unfortunate enough to be attached to it. "I'll cut it off, just like that!" she insisted. "I won't think twice." Their sex life and the man's sleep were both disturbed for a certain length of time. But from that moment on, he was courteous to a fault with her and, until the end, she heard nothing from him but irreproachably romantic words of love. Two months later, Marie-Angèle realised she was pregnant; she was nearly thirty. The Légionnaire was giddy with happiness and dared not protest when Marie-Angèle declared there was no chance that the baby would have any other name but Susini. "Anyway, it's like you don't even have a name," she pointed out to him. "I bet you don't even remember what your name was when you came into this world!" He had to admit she was right. Until Virginie turned three, he was an excellent father, loving and present, whenever his military duties allowed, and no doubt he would have continued that way had he not been killed in Chad, or in a Shiite village in Lebanon, one or the other, in 1979 or 1980. "I spent more than ten years of my life with him," Marie-Angèle would say. "I believe he loved me in the end.

I don't even know what his mother tongue was." She was so sad she left Calvi and returned to the family house emptied by death, exile and shame. She spent part of her savings making the place liveable, redecorating it in order to harry out all the pushy ghosts that Stéphane Campana's arrival had awoken several years later, as she had always feared. With the money that remained, she reopened the village bar, closed for eons. She hired waitresses, which was not very hard. Any number of lost girls from just about everywhere came carrying their desperate baggage from the city, in search of some kind of work. Being hired by Marie-Angèle was the best thing that could happen to them. Militant nationalists faithfully patronised the bar and were quick to make it their headquarters. The drunks who might have tried to take advantage of the absence of a male boss to harass Marie-Angèle or her barmaids were quickly dissuaded. Vincent watched over them. He returned from his travels with a desperate, protective love of fallen girls. He would not tolerate any lack of respect for them. Marie-Angèle could devote herself to Virginie; she devoted herself to her with all her soul and with ever-increasing worry as she watched her grow into a deep, dreamy girl, as if nature had programmed her to be the victim of the first scoundrel who came along, and all the love of a perfect upbringing could change nothing, which was confirmed beyond a shadow of a doubt that horrible summer evening when Marie-Angèle caught her allowing herself to be voluptuously sullied by the intent and shameless look that Stéphane Campana was giving her. Marie-Angèle's life had been simple, monotonous, even, the kind of life others feel it is their right to look down on, the way I would have at the age of twenty, or thirty, or forty too, most likely. But I knew then that it was an honourable life, completely centred on an unshakable idea of dignity and certainty, and that fidelity to that idea had infinitely more importance than the circles under her eyes, her hands ruined by dishwater, the early wrinkles, the humble jobs, and the condescending looks from people who, like me, have never understood that an idea can be important.

I have such a memory overload – but I still remember the way, when I was younger, that Borges remark about Richard Burton struck me. He said Burton had tried "all the ways of being a man that men know", and I pictured those words as the great emblem of my future life. I never profaned the Kaaba with my clandestine presence among the pious crowd of believers, not a single Sudanese lance pierced my cheeks, I never translated *The Thousand and One Nights* nor wrote a treatise on swordplay, and I never discovered the terrifying headwaters of the Nile. My experiments were limited, sadly enough, to the multiple ways of being the same man. And the most emblematic scene of my life that has played out hundreds of times is this: I am pitifully averting my eyes as a woman, a different one each time, but always with tears of rage, is calling me a son of a bitch. The only thing I have always succeeded at is fucking frenetically. I fucked all the girls at university who were naive enough to be interested in me for my intellectual capabilities and my manipulative gift of listening, and later, in the Venezuelan sector of the Amazon basin, I worked my way through most of the girls in the tribe of ugly creatures about whom I was supposed to be writing a monograph, before returning to France and using the incredible success of that monograph in the university microcosm to fuck my girl students and colleagues until I finally succeeded in becoming, justifiably, an object of hatred for my wife and children, my life becoming so complicated and empty that I ended up torpedoing my career by accepting a post at the University of Corsica, where I immediately set about fucking my new colleagues, my new girl students, and a good swathe of the administrative staff. Of course, it didn't take long before my exploits made me an object of disgust in the eyes of everyone who knew me, and I soon found myself alone in my house in Corte with the ghost of a dismal colonel and follower of Pascal Paoli who died in 1769 and answered to the name of Gianfranco de Lanfranchi. I never knew if he was a real ghost, or, as the doctors almost convinced me later at the Castelluccio psychiatric hospital, merely the chatty manifestation of my guilt. I was interned for nearly two years a few weeks after I admitted, half-way through a university reception, in a fit of fake sincerity that was, I fear, just another of my outpourings of bullshit, that I was an impostor, that the monograph that had made me famous was a tissue of lies, like all my books that were published afterwards and that set down, with greater self-assurance and self-weariness, those same lies. But no-one would believe me and, still today, *Creative Perception* (modestly subtitled *An Ontology of the Ti-Gwaï Nation*) is for students of ethnology a work nearly as essential as *Tristes Tropiques*. After I exited the hospital, with nowhere else to go, I settled in my father's old house with a supply of pills, a medical follow-up, and a disability pension, in this village that was empty of childhood memories where Marie-Angèle seemed to be awaiting me. At the beginning, the solitude was so intolerable that I came close to halting my treatment in the hope that Gianfranco would appear once again so I could continue our discussions. I thought back to those conversations with abominable nostalgia. I dreamed of him. I heard the suave, unhealthy tone of his voice. I felt, as he had once suggested to me, that he was the only person I had ever loved. I began to think of my wife and children with the hope that one day I might see them again. Yet I still felt the nostalgia for things that never existed.

I became aware of my memory problems not long after my arrival in Corte. I was in bed with a teaching assistant in modern literature. The week before, on my return from a few days in Paris, I had come across her in the library and said hello. She looked at me, ecstasy in her eyes, and whispered, "You know,

Théodore, it's terrible to go days without seeing you . . ." Then she blushed and left me standing there, completely taken aback, not knowing what to do. The very next day, I invited her to a restaurant and soon she was in my bed where I recalled with some emotion (mixed with arrogance) her artless confession. "What you said to me in the library was really touching," I told her. "What did I say?" she asked. When I repeated her words, she burst out laughing and claimed she never would have said such a silly thing. I was at a loss. I pictured her, and heard her with perfect clarity. Yet when I thought about it, how was it possible, when I heard her declaration, that I had been taken aback, at a loss, the way I remembered? If a woman had told me something of the sort, I would have known what to do right off, I would not have let her get away, I would have fucked her then and there, among the stacks if necessary. I had dreamed it all up, and it had unfortunately managed to slip into my memory as if it had really occurred, if the word *really* has any meaning. If what we dream fits perfectly and coherently into the course of our everyday life, then how can we differentiate the memory of a dream and the memory of a real event? In the weeks that followed, I tried to verify discreetly the validity of several other memories, appealing to the individuals concerned, and discovered that at least half my memories were not attached to any reality. I did not understand straight away the significance of my memory overload. At the beginning I was happy not to give much credence to what I remembered, which played tricks on me, notably during the Master's thesis defence of one of my female students. She was speaking and it seemed to me that I had several times dreamed that I was in bed with her. I pictured her giving in to my demands with an eagerness that had something academic about it. As I was about to take the floor as chairman of the jury, I dismissed my erotic thoughts and pointed out in a harsh tone that her work was, in a word, sloppy, that she had not even taken the trouble to adequately reread her dissertation, the proof being the many typos that were still present, not to mention the spelling mistakes. She began to cry, which was the normal thing to do, but then she gave me a look of pure hatred and started screaming like a hysteric, playing for her own advantage, and to perfection, the scene I knew so well. "You bastard!" she cried. "I didn't have the time to fix my dissertation because I was in bed with you! You swore it didn't matter and that you wouldn't hold it against me! You said I'd get an excellent grade!" The other jury members had the good taste to escort her out of the room and pretend they believed me when I assured them we were in the presence of an emotionally disturbed person. After the incident, I decided it was wise to keep material proof of everything that happened to me or, failing that, at least take notes so I could compare my memories with something tangible. This was a particularly painful decision, but the only feasible one. I could not make up my mind to consult a psychiatrist, first because I was never able to fit them in, and then because Gianfranco had begun to appear, and I suspected that if I revealed the entire list of my problems, I would not be allowed to simply waltz out of the office. I hate archives. Signing a cheque is something I prefer to avoid. The idea that some insignificant scraps of paper could outlive me has long been a source of anxiety, and, despite the benefits I have derived from them, I have never forgiven myself for writing books. I must have accumulated kilograms of paper notes, on which I wrote down things as uninteresting as the atmosphere of my conversations and the names of people I happened to meet. I could have related only important facts, but how can anyone know ahead of time what will be important? Sometimes, when the act became too absurd, I stopped writing anything at all. But the fear of seeing my past change before my eyes sent me back to note-taking. I also began a collection of women's panties that had nothing to do with any tendency towards fetishism. I persuaded my conquests to surrender their precious garments on a salacious or romantic pretext, or I pinched the item in question, then inscribed the date and the name of its proprietress – which allowed me to replay a variation of my favourite scene the day one of my mistresses found the box in which I kept them, and threw the contents in my face, calling me a bastard. I had pretty much reached an acceptable solution, only to ask myself the question that nearly made me lose what little reason remained: since when had I been suffering from memory overload? And what had my life been?

I had no doubts about my work in the Amazon: in my book, and even in my living room, there were photographs of me posing with those primitive Ti-Gwaï creatures. But what about Ruth and the children? I remembered, it seemed, that when I left them, in my feverish need to begin a new life, I eliminated all photographs and other documents. I threw away the divorce papers. As I recall, Ruth refused to stoop to asking me for alimony and even served notice that she would not accept a penny from me. If I did not want to be the father of my children, she would make sure my wish was fulfilled. They would live only in my lying memory. I was able to explain the fact that I retained no palpable remnant of them, but what was that explanation worth? Our brain is a machine that fabricates coherent stories; that is what it does, at all times. Perhaps we are no more than a coherent story. Possibly, I protected my false memory by fabricating other memories, just as false. For a time, I was relieved to have found a solution that would put an end to my doubts: I would ask for a copy of my complete identification records. My marriage would be noted there. But I never did it. I did not want to risk discovering that everything was fake, I did not want to lose them again, and in the most definitive way imaginable, I did not want all possibility of return to be destroyed once and for all, even if I knew there would be no return, I did not want, among the other losses, to lose Sarah, my daughter, whose face I pictured with such clarity, I did not want my daughter to disappear into nothingness. Perhaps I experience terrible nostalgia for things that do not exist. But I do not want to lose that nostalgia.

I never asked for a copy of my records. I continued to think of them as real people. During the beginning of my time in the village, unable to fall asleep in the empty house, I thought of those nights when I would awake and listen to Ruth breathing next to me. Softly I would press up against her, I would wrap myself around her to escape my anxiety. I felt that all life had been extinguished, we were drifting together in a universe frozen in silence, and without her I would be completely alone, falling through night – the way I made sure I would do now. I spent the greater part of my days at the bar, drinking mineral water and watching Hayet moving her long tired hands in the dishwater. At the beginning, I did not talk to Vincent who was always there, at the end of the bar. Later in the afternoon, Marie-Angèle would show up. The place got a little livelier. I started talking to them. To Hayet. And Vincent. And then Marie-Angèle. We began talking to each other at length. About myself, I first told her what seemed decent (in other words, not much) and then, without knowing why, as if my two years in the psychiatric hospital had really amounted to something, I told the whole truth, including the fact that I could not guarantee it was the truth. That was on an evening when I was having dinner at her house. For the first time she lay her hand on my cheek. I asked her, "Is that the first time? I feel like you've done that a thousand times." She did not answer. She touched my cheek again and said I could spend the night with her if I wanted. In a wave of uncontrollable sincerity, I admitted that my last erection dated back to 1994, a few weeks before I entered the asylum, when psychotropic and anxiolytic drugs deprived me of what had been the sole point of interest in my life, and the sole source of regret. "It's not about that, you know," she told me. I felt immersed in tenderness and gratitude.

During the four years I spent in the village, I crossed paths several times with Stéphane Campana on his way to see Virginie, which he continued to do on a regular basis even once he was married. His courtesy was almost as irreproachable as when I first met him, and came to know him quite well, in Corte, when he was leading the student union, and would often ask my advice about his history thesis. Back then our encounters, most of which were of a professional nature, were carefully noted down in a little book. I could see that my stay in the psychiatric hospital had been fatal to the respect he, like most of the university community, had shown me. It was not much, a suspicion of condescension, a degree of extra formality, courteous contempt, nothing really offensive. I never had reason to complain about him, and when I stepped past his corpse, it was with a twinge of regret. There is something mysterious about seeing someone you have known as a living being, whose voice and expressions you remember, reduced to the condition of pure matter, like a wax mannequin. I should have felt something more But I suppose that, with time, I had adopted Marie-Angèle's opinion of Stéphane, and it kept me from further emotion about his death. The corpse had been carted away. In Ajaccio, the forensic specialist would have used thick thread to sew up the Y-shaped incision he had inflicted on the dead man's torso to extract each of the organs, cutting them into sections and weighing them, after he had opened the sternum with shears and lopped off the top of his cranium with a circular saw. Next to the examining table, there must have been a shiny silver dish full of fragments of bloody bullets. A betrayed wife wept with pain and humiliation. And Marie-Angèle felt the breath of life return.

Her daughter's liaison had lasted nine years and had exhausted Marie-Angèle, but she had remained true to herself. She never gave up hope that one day Virginie would recover some sense of pride and realise that love was not compatible with the way Stéphane Campana treated her – something Marie-Angèle viscerally believed. She knew there was no use telling the girl as much; she would have to make the painful discovery on her own. She would be there to console her daughter and show her, as she did discreetly, tirelessly, every day, what real love was. She did not care for idle chatter (the people of the village, whose malevolent memory was accurate in all things, immediately leaped to the conclusion that her daughter's precocious moral depravity was caused by the infallible action of a mysterious whorish gene inherited from her retarded grandmother). She was interested only in the self-respect Virginie owed herself and that she had so passionately sacrificed. "Not only does he not love her, that bastard," Marie-Angèle would tell me, "but he doesn't even bother pretending he respects her." One day she found a scrapbook in Virginie's room in which her daughter had pasted all the newspaper articles that mentioned Stéphane Campana's political activities and all the photographs of him that had been published, photographs taken at rallies, demonstrations and on the sets of the local television channels. There were also underground press conferences. Reading the date of the first article, Marie-Angèle realised Virginie had begun her work of hagiography when she was no more than ten years old. "What can you do about that kind of obsession?" she asked me. During the troubles in 1995, Virginie had scrupulously noted the dates of the murders with the victims' names, she had cut out the photographs of bodies, and she must have taken advantage of the chaos after the murder of Dominique Guerrini to take a picture of him, bent double in the fearful attitude of a child trying to escape a nightmare, gunned down as he left the village bar. And now all that was over. Marie-Angèle imagined a brighter future and let herself go with me, with total confidence, now that the raging monster inside me had been exterminated by repeated doses of lithium. "And you know the worst thing, Théodore?" she asked. "The worst thing was that she didn't love him either. The thing she was so mad about, even if she didn't realise it, was a dream she'd made up on her own, a dream that imprisoned her. That's all it was."

Forgetting must settle in and surprise us. Marie-Angèle hoped Virginie would continue to cry, and go on wanting to die, and then all that would gently fade, she would understand she had the right to be happy, or at least to try to be, for human beings are condemned to that pursuit. Perhaps she would even convince herself that was what the dead man wanted, for her to start a new life that he would give his blessing to from the great hereafter, and be happy for her. I had no doubt that would happen. Yet I knew, since I had cohabited at length with a ghost, that the dead are not happy for us. They do not give us their blessing. They resent that we are still alive. They hate us and they are jealous of us. If they hold back from hurting us, it is only because they desperately need our memory, that imperfect labyrinth, to survive a little longer, safe from the dreams of young girls, their toxic powers and their spells.

"BEHIND YOU, THE SEA . . ."

K haled told me this story:

Tariq ibn Ziyad never burned his boats off the coast of Spain. He claimed he did, so divine things would remain concealed. The truth is that he had no boats. He had no need of them. God pulled the sea tight before him so he could gallop across it and our fathers might follow him. He galloped past the rock that today bears his name, kicking up sea-foam as he went. He galloped along the beach. And when the hoof of the last horse of the last warrior of Islam struck the sands of Andalusia, God drew back his hand. The miracle was over. For God, who sees into the heart of man, withdrew His hand and the sea became shifting and deep for all eternity so that no-one can turn back. It has stayed that way until this day. But now conquests, not retreats, are forbidden us. The victorious warriors fell back like a stone thrown into the air. We had been cast so very high – in truth, so high, my sister, so high we could not imagine it! – only to fall back into shit.

And now we are here, both of us. We are walking along Balco Atlantico and Khaled lays his hand on my shoulder. We watch the sun sink into the ocean as he invents a new story for me. He lights a joint and I will get two or three puffs, no more.

Look around and tell me, Hayet, what do you see? People like to go walking here because the horizon goes on forever. But what do you see, in truth? The ocean is a wall, we are surrounded by walls. There are walls of water, and walls of sand. We are always on the wrong side. But nowhere is it written that we must stay here forever. Do not believe it is written somewhere, for only God knows what is written. It is for us to discover. Why would it be written that for all time I must wake up at two in the morning like Father and my older brothers, and bust my ass fishing to make just enough to survive on? Is it also written that your life will resemble Mother's or our sister Karima's, and that you will lose your beauty under the roof of a man who will make you pregnant and then be too exhausted to speak the slightest word to you? What could I do for you then? Why would God desire such a thing? In what way would this be holy? When I leave, you will come with me.

Yes, of course, I will come. But not because I am afraid of turning into Mother or Karima. It is because I do not want to live far away from him.

Two weeks ago, our parents said they were going to see our sister in Rabat. Mother seemed uncomfortable. Khaled and I were alone in the house. We were in his room listening to music. He smoked an enormous amount. Our father is like many old people: every evening he smokes a pipe of kif and plays cards in the medina, but he will not tolerate joints. We should have been aware of his suspicions. An hour later, the door to the room opened; we had heard nothing. Father was standing there, staring at us. The room was full of sweet-smelling fog. Khaled was holding a joint. Father looked at him and said nothing, then motioned to me to leave. Then he closed the door again and left my brother alone, petrified with fear. He has not spoken to him since. He did not hit him. He has not reproached him. He simply acts as though he does not exist. I know that Khaled will leave and I will leave with him.

But you know, Hayet, we won't go to Tangiers for visas. We won't stand in line all day in front of the French consulate and be treated like shit by those dogs. They can treat me like shit, I will bend over and take it, but at least give me a visa. But they'll never give us one. They'll take our money to open a file, those bastards, then they'll tell us no, it's always no. We'll have to do it another way. We'll have to get to Spain on a boat, with a smuggler. I wrote to Uncle Hassan and I'm sure he'll help us. I'll make the money we need, you'll see.

Every morning, Khaled goes into the city to look for tourists who might need a guide. He speaks pretty good French, English and Spanish, and even a little German. He takes them to the ruins of the Roman town. He tells them, as he tells me, fascinating things that never occurred. He escorts them through the alleyways of the medina. He asks them about their country and he remembers everything. When he can, he sells them some hash. It is easy because many of them have come just for that. Now he is saving all the money he makes. He is determined. He is not thinking about what he will leave behind. Or what might be awaiting him there. My mother says that, from the day he was born, she could see he would never be happy, it was the way he opened his eyes to the world. He was marked by something, sadness or ingratitude, she was not sure. Something that would keep him from appreciating what God offered him. She hoped it was sadness. For sadness is a disgrace, but ingratitude is a sin.

You know, Hayet, maybe it is true that Tariq's warriors used boats to cross over to Spain. But God helped them one way or other, of course.

A YOUNG GIRL'S DREAM

(1985–91)

Vincent Leandri loved them, and, because he did, he tolerated their excessive attention and the constant burden of their admiration. Years earlier, when he returned from the Indian Ocean, he felt only incomprehension and contempt for them. Their actions seemed so stupid and self-destructive that he could feel no compassion for them. They were backward, arrogant teenagers, so poorly suited for life they deserved what happened to them. And then, softly at first but ever more distinctly, in the soughing of the waves, in the silence of the villages in winter, in the bars where they shouted for another round, in their hysterical gesticulations, he began to hear the beating of a deep dark heart, a maleficent heart carrying waves of sadness and boredom that, desperately, unknowing, they were trying to escape. Consider this: one of them, for months, amused himself by barking at the gendarmes of the Olmiccia detachment. He watched for them when they drove across the village square, then ran after their vehicle, barking and slobbering like a dog. When he spotted their trademark blue Renault 4L parked at the side of the road for an identity check, he would creep up quietly, bent low so as not to be seen in the side-view mirror, then leap up next to the door, barking *Arf! Arf! Arf!* in the terrified driver's ear, then run away laughing like a madman. When a cop full of goodwill tried to fraternise with the locals by stopping off for a coffee at the café, he would yelp plaintively from the back of the room, then bound over and sniff the cop's jacket with a mournful air as it lay on the counter. Beyond a few sidelong glances, the cops did nothing until one day they arrested him and marched him to the Ajaccio courthouse because he had barked at them one time too many, offering them two marijuana plants bought for the express purpose of getting on their nerves. In the same way, another of the guys and his brother decided to knock over a gas station using a motorbike, and after leaving his fingerprints everywhere because he had forgotten his gloves, slipped on an oily spot as he was making his getaway. A third guy came up with the great idea of losing his wallet with all his papers in perfect order on the way out of a bar that he had held up in Ajaccio. They all ended up in front of a judge who sent them off to prison after trying in vain to understand them, suspecting that the most accomplished stupidity, the purest imbecility, could not explain such inept actions whose chances of success had been sabotaged with meticulous care and a kind of catastrophic genius. The judge gazed at them with disbelief and each held his gaze silently, not because they concealed treasures of unspeakable depth, but because they had nothing to say. A few months later, a sports car came speeding up and swerved in front of the bar, raising a plume of dust and, with it, hilarious cries of triumph from one of them who had just been freed. He kissed everyone, Marie-Angèle Susini, the waitresses, the customers, he ordered rounds for the house and could not stop talking, describing the glories of prison with great peals of laughter, struggling secretly and in vain to bury his terror in forgetfulness, to deafen his ears to the echo of the heavy locks snapping shut that awoke him with a start every morning and would go on making him jump in the middle of the night, forgetting the pillow he had bitten down on to keep from crying in front of his fellow inmates the first time the door swung shut on him, to forget his childish terrors, his prayers and his loneliness.

During one of those episodes, the complete exasperation Vincent felt at all that public declamation and childish ostentation turned into affection. Despite himself, he began to feel part of a family. And it was true: those men were his family. Maybe he too had been trying to escape the beatings of a secret heart he had not yet heard back when he left for the Indian Ocean. What was the point of it? Everything he had undertaken between Madagascar, Mayotte and the Comoro Islands, from growing sacred *zamal* to trading in Madagascan pottery and trafficking in shark fins, had been an utter failure. He resigned himself to not having been born at the right time. The 1930s would have suited him better, he could have been a military officer, or an adventurer, a swash-buckler, something that would have satisfied his incorrigible romanticism, but he came into this world after the colonial empire was dead. The tropical sun shone only upon disaster. No-one could do anything about it, no sense bucking the tide, though it had taken him years to understand. Years of humidity and heat and frightening excess, with plants that grew overnight like tumours, the multi-hued swarming of insects that tumbled into the open collar of his shirt and laid eggs under his skin, fruits with perfumes so heady they induced nausea, years of tropical poxes and rashes and mycosis, years of knocking back litres of rum so disgusting the drinker had to marinate some kind of crap in it, anything, vanilla, centipedes, or rotten mangos, it was months before he could drink it, then go to bed with girls who hated him. He did not suspect such hatred existed until it appeared to him in all the evidence of its simplicity the night he awoke at two o'clock in the morning and caught the girl he had picked up in a bar in Mamoudzou crawling furtively through the dark room, grabbing everything she could, money, cigarettes, stamps, everything. In flagrante did not ruffle her. Instead of begging his pardon, she insulted him in a language he had not bothered to learn, then spat on him. He could not blame her. He let her leave with everything she wanted and more. He was white; therefore, he was rich. The girls were black, and poor. There was no more to say. A week later, after waking up by the side of a road with a splitting hangover, next to the garbage dump where a contemplative zebu was chewing on a plastic bag and watching him with a bovine look, he decided to return to Corsica.

Strangely, freed from his illusions and dreams of distant travel, he felt better. He was happy to rediscover the village that he had fled with such disgust. He was ready to accept being what he was. He met up with Dominique Guerrini, his childhood friend, who had just finished his second stay in prison, and helped him organise the nationalist movement that was rapidly expanding in the region. Years before, he would not have lifted a finger for a political cause. But now he had become attentive to the deep beating of a heart, and he felt sadness spreading in all directions. In these lost young men, he saw brothers in need of help. And he could help them: he could give them something to believe in without ridicule, he could fill their lives with something that, for the first time, had meaning. He overcame Dominique's reticence and recruited a dozen such young men, and, after a trial period, turned them into an underground movement. The F.L.N.C. enjoyed extraordinary prestige. In June 1984, on the T.V. set at the bar, everyone looked wide-eyed at the militants who had been arrested after the attack on Ajaccio prison. They radiated strength and youth, walking with their heads high and their eyes proud as the policemen took them away, and everyone watched as they brandished their handcuffs that sparkled in the sunlight like the bracelets kings might wear, bracelets of pure gold. To a population fascinated by its own failure and all forms of martyrdom and magnificent defeat, the cameras showed men full of courage and abnegation, sacrificing their freedom for an ideal of justice, and no-one doubted it was superior to the law. The young men of the village received permission to wear a balaclava, and they were infinitely grateful. They felt greater and nobler in the light of clandestine existence, and looked upon Vincent and Dominique as their benefactors. No-one barked at the cops or felt the need to dream up totally inept robberies. They had become devoted, faithful, lost in admiration. They were swimming in happiness.

That evening Vincent spotted a young man he had never seen before leaning on the bar next to Tony Versini. His head was shaved and he wore a timid look. Vincent smiled and raised his glass and the young man looked away, blushing.

"You know that kid?" Vincent asked Dominique.

Dominique shook his head.

"Tony!" Vincent called. "Aren't you going to introduce your friend?"

Tony came over immediately, followed by the young man. Vincent asked him his name.

"Stéphane Campana."

He and Vincent shook hands. Then it was Dominique

Guerrini's turn, above the glasses of crystallised pastis. He rubbed Stéphane's skull with his fingertips.

"Did you do that to your hair on purpose? Do you think it's cute, or was it a dare?"

Tony laughed on cue, and Stéphane blushed a deeper red.

"Neither. I just got out of the service. I'm going to let it grow back."

"Stéphane wanted to meet you," Tony said. "That's why I brought him here."

"If you want to make our acquaintance, don't stand there like a couple of idiots at the end of the bar," Vincent told them.

Stéphane's ears turned crimson.

"Come on," Vincent said, kindly. "What are you having? Marie-Angèle will pour us a drink and we'll get acquainted."

They talked, and Stéphane felt more comfortable. He spoke of his convictions and desire for involvement. For the first time in his life, divine grace had turned its eyes in his direction. Then a wave of nausea rose up inside him, it was the harbinger of a migraine, something he had suffered from since childhood. He excused himself, said he needed some fresh air, he would be right back. Outside, he breathed in the warm August evening greedily, and prayed the headache would spare him. He breathed slowly, his eyes closed. Not now, he told himself, not tonight, not now. The nausea subsided, then faded. When Stéphane opened his eyes in relief, he saw the little girl. She was sitting on a stone wall and looking at him so intensely, so seriously, that he immediately felt embarrassed. He tried to smile, and asked her who she was. She did not return his smile, but answered in a husky voice, pronouncing each word deliberately. "That's my Mama's bar. My name is Virginie and I'm seven years old." Her hair was long and tangled like a witch's. She sized him up through her long quivering eyelashes. He turned on his heel and all but ran back to the bar to join those he hoped would soon be his friends.

Stéphane had a nationalist streak, and, like everyone, he admired Vincent greatly and Dominique more. But he had another motivation. Political involvement would give him the chance to work for an ideal he believed in, while hopefully relieving him of the virginity that still afflicted him at the age of twenty-one. He had noticed that militancy had a remarkable and totally irrational effect on girls. A week earlier, he had received irrefutable proof of that fact when Tony Versini (who was neither handsome nor intelligent and whom Stéphane considered the stupidest person he had ever met, and a loud-mouth on top of it), that dim-witted Tony Versini, right before his very eyes, took home two girls at once. He had let on to these two Italian girls, as he puffed himself up, that he was an important person in politics, and supported his assertion by exhibiting, right there in the nightclub, a hand grenade and a Desert Eagle so enormous he could hardly fit it into his pants. The girls squealed with admiration, asked to touch the weapon, and fell in behind Tony the minute he asked them to, leaving Stéphane alone with his resentment in the booth. The fact that women, those beings for whom he felt such adoration, could be seduced by such vulgar and stupid tactics the way those Italians had been, whereas they paid no attention to him – that cast him into the depths of incomprehension and despair. He did not stand a chance. After secondary school, he studied history at the University of Nice, and waited for the love affairs to begin. But the day after he arrived, during a brawl that did not even concern him, he took a punch straight to the nose, a right hand that was not meant for him. His face immediately swelled up and for the next two weeks he was disfigured by a pair of enormous black eyes. Among the girl students from Corsica, he was finished. And he knew only people from Corsica. Life in Nice became so intolerable that he answered the call early and left to do his military service. He was stationed at the Corte regional establishment in charge of materiel, where he quickly understood that a fulfilling sex life was incompatible with a uniform. He regretted he had not been sent somewhere north – like the Vosges, why not? Another example that life was unfair. The University of Corsica had reopened its doors two years earlier in an atmosphere of intense political fervour, and the students considered that anyone who wore a uniform was a stooge of the French national state. They were absolutely not willing to see the difference between career soldiers and those called up to serve, though the latter were clearly victims of the state, not its supporters. Stéphane had to put up with hateful looks and exasperated sighs that he could not ignore. When he went out in street clothes, his shaved head betrayed him, and he ended up on his own, or hanging out with pariahs like himself. Yet he was Corsican, he had been born in Corsica and spoke the language, unlike a lot of the students who grew up in Paris suburbs like Sarcelles or God-knows-where, and had signed up at Corte for militant reasons, and spoke with horrible Parisian accents, yet still managed to notch up the conquests.

Stéphane understood that his real problem was not his objective bad luck but the strength of his desire, his attitude of adoration. He loved girls so much he was petrified when he saw one. When they came near, he lost his mind. It was not love in the usual meaning of the word (he never thought of meeting the woman of his dreams and marrying her), but neither was it pure lust. Though the idea of possessing a woman obsessed him constantly, painfully, he was not prone to solitary pleasure. There was something else, some ecstatic fervour, an illumination or mystical drive towards the flesh. In summer, he spent his days on the beach, watching women. They wore brightly coloured bikini bottoms, and the elastic bands wore deep furrows where their thighs came together, and from time to time they would lift the fabric, and he would catch a fleeting glance of tight curls turned golden by the sun. The warm breeze stiffened their nipples when they emerged from the sea and sprinted, trickling water, towards the little thatched shelters where they would eat ice cream that melted quickly. Frozen drops would fall on their tanned stomachs, and they would cry out in delight and surprise, and sometimes, when the melted ice cream dropped onto their wrist, they would stick out the pink tip of their tongues and lap it up with hungry laughter. In painful, stultified meditation, Stéphane would contemplate the salty lines on their tanned skin. It was monstrous torture, this horrible profusion of youth and beauty, too much to give him a hard-on, he felt a cauldron of frustration and celestial desire boiling in his chest, as if his body contained an erupting volcano. It was unbearable. They were there, steps away, and Stéphane was petrified. Which one should he talk to? Which one should he choose? Each was more beautiful than the next, the blonds, the brunettes, the black women, the Arabs, big or small or round, he discovered a particular miraculous and unique form of beauty in each of them, each shone in her own way. When he cast his eyes on one among the crowd, he immediately spotted another, and ended up glued to his chair. He faced the world and all that beauty like Buridan's ass, only in heat, a total carnal, spiritual heat that consumed his soul.

Back in the bar, he forgot about the little girl. His nausea had disappeared. No migraine in sight. He drank and talked and felt more at ease and saw that Vincent and Dominique appreciated what he had to say. "Alright," Vincent said, putting on his jacket, "we're going, but we'll see each other again soon. Summer's almost over and the meetings will be starting up again next week in the back room. You'd be welcome. We'll count on you." Stéphane felt new life opening up before him. He wanted to give Tony a kiss. From outside, her face pressed against the glass door, the little girl was watching him. He turned around and saw her. He was in such a good mood he sent her a friendly wave. She answered by opening her mouth in a wide surprised circle.

Stéphane soon made himself indispensable with the local section of the movement. He wrote several reports on the meetings, and his style attracted Vincent's praise. He was then given the job of writing notes on various cultural and political subjects, and these were judged to be perfect. "Get a look at this, you bunch of illiterates!" Vincent laughed. The other guys lowered their heads and smiled, dejected at being illiterates but happy to be the objects of affectionate teasing. Winter had settled in and Stéphane's political life was almost idyllic. He came down from Corte on Fridays and conscientiously prepared the weekend meetings. But two things continued to worry him. For starters, he was still as much a virgin as he had been before he became a militant. The few girls in his section seemed to appreciate his pen, but not his person. But since he did not dare speak to them, he had no way of proving his hypothesis. And second, no-one had asked him to be part of the F.L.N.C. If the latter problem was resolved, he was sure, the former would immediately follow, and he was more than impatient for that to happen. One December evening, after adjourning the meeting, Vincent leaned over and spoke into Stéphane's ear. "Stay a couple minutes after," he said. Stéphane would long remember the silence of the empty room and the wild beating of his heart as he waited for Dominique and Vincent.

They told him he was a good guy, both of them thought so, that he was intelligent and honest, and best of all he didn't talk nonsense. The same couldn't be said for some of the others. Stéphane nodded his appreciation, swallowing hard under this torrent of praise. Was he ready to make himself useful in other ways, now, was he ready, they asked him more than once.

"Yes, of course, for sure. You bet! You can't imagine how long I've waited," he answered.

Dominique looked doubtful.

"It's not a game, my friend. We're not inviting you to a masked ball, you understand?"

Stéphane reassumed his veneer of calmness and mute acquiescence.

"Alright, then! Meet us here next Monday at eight o'clock, O.K.?"

"And you'll get a balaclava," Vincent added.

Stéphane savoured the moment.

"Are you going to give me a gun?" he asked.

"You think we're a bunch of girl guides?" Vincent chuckled.

"We have weapons for the operations, but if you want your own gun, you'll have to buy it. But don't get carried away! We didn't choose you for your warrior instincts. We need guys with brains. Forget about guns for now. O.K., we're finished here!"

But Stéphane wanted a pistol. The business about brains and warrior instincts bothered him. Why couldn't he be a warrior and have a brain as well? His new status as an underground militant would not be complete if he did not carry a gun. And he wanted one before Monday's meeting. He told Tony about his aspirations, and he offered to lend him an old P38 that his grandfather had stolen from a German officer when he returned from the *stalag* where he spent the duration of the war. But Stéphane would have no part of it. Tony told him he would see if there was something for sale, and Stéphane dipped deeply into his student loan. On Saturday, Tony informed him that he had located something. The little girl was drinking grenadine syrup by herself at a table, and, in her serious way, she asked Stéphane for a kiss. He went to her and kissed her on the forehead. Very quickly she threw her arms around his neck to return the kiss, then pulled away. "Virginie, is that it?" he asked, stroking her hair. When she heard her name spoken, she broke out in a luminous smile.

Away from prying eyes, Tony opened a bag and took out two loaded clips, bullets, and then, finally, a Colt. 45 wrapped in a rag. Stéphane appreciated its venomous beauty. A strange power of lethal seduction rose off it, almost as irresistible as the one the Desert Eagle had displayed. He paid Tony, loaded his weapon, and stuck it in his belt. When he sat down behind the wheel, he felt the barrel digging into his crotch. There was no danger (there was no bullet in the chamber and the safety was on), but it was extremely uncomfortable. He pulled on the grip so the barrel would not penetrate so deeply into the unsounded mysteries of his pants. A few kilometres out of the village, too late, he saw lights by the side of the road. It was a police roadblock. He pulled over, trying not to panic. He knew the police could not perform a body search, so there was no problem. Soon he would have to keep his cool in situations a lot more dangerous than this. Fate was offering a risk-free rehearsal, a way of testing his self-control. He handed his papers to the policeman through the open window. A minute later, he was asked to open the trunk.

"Of course," Stéphane said eagerly, and opened the car door with the same eagerness.

He stepped out and stood up. He performed that ordinary act, then heard a soft thud and suddenly felt lighter. The Colt was lying in the dust, in the light of the policeman's flashlight. Stéphane looked into the gendarme's eyes: he was slowly drawing his gun from his holster.

"Whatever you do, kid, don't move."

Stéphane could not have moved if he had wanted to.

*

During that first night in Ajaccio jail, his face pressed against his pillow like so many before him, Stéphane wanted to die. For a guy with brains, he was pretty stupid, he thought, and he cursed himself. His arrest was completely ridiculous. He had not been thinking. What had he needed a pistol for? He should have listened to Vincent instead of acting like a child. But it was too late. He'd never get a second chance to convince Vincent and Dominique that he was ready to listen to them from now on, and be less of a fool. They would never speak to him again, and they would be right. He deserved their contempt. He thought of Virginie's smile. It was the only source of beauty that had ever brightened his dull, grotesque existence. The obvious truth of his failure crushed him against the stinking mattress.

He was sentenced to three months in prison. A few days later, he was surprised to see his name on the list of political prisoners published by a nationalist newspaper. In the visiting room the next day, his mother did not show up, but Vincent Leandri did. He did not seem angry, or in any hurry to make fun of him. Instead, he gave him a look of great compassion. When Stéphane felt Vincent's hand on his arm, when he heard his voice asking if he needed anything, he clenched his jaw with all his might but could not keep a tear from dropping onto the table. After the visit was over, he returned to his cell full of new vitality. He stopped dreading the coming weeks. He had not lost anything after all. He could feel the distant warmth of other lights. He was still in prison when, in January 1986, the F.L.N.C. took credit for killing two Tunisian drug dealers.

Within the nationalist movement, there was considerable conflict. For the first time, Vincent and Dominique had a serious disagreement as their confused foot soldiers looked on silently. Though Vincent Leandri was duly admired, Dominique Guerrini, thanks to his warrior past attested to by two prison sentences, was the object of true veneration. Still, Dominique did not like violence, though he knew that something profoundly rotten in the hearts of men often made it necessary: the perverse inability to resolve problems through reason, a repugnant and base love of brute force, the ignoble mark of sin. At eighteen, he had married Vannina, his first love. In the village, he looked after a small-scale farm, and she worked as a monitor in the college in town and took correspondence courses. After he had caught her crying in the bathroom several times, he forced her to confess: she had been the victim of constant harassment from her vice-principal. "Why?" Dominique wanted to know, and she said she had no idea. Her distress broke Dominique's heart. "I'll go and talk to him if you like," he offered, but she cried even harder and said it was no use, it would only make things worse. "You'll see," Dominique promised her. "There must be some misunderstanding." The next day, he went to the college. The vice-principal was filing documents in the photocopy room. Without looking up from the task at hand, he silenced Dominique with a curt wave of his hand as he was politely introducing himself. "Wait till I've finished, young man!" After five long minutes, he finally looked in his direction and with a nod of his chin gave him permission to speak. Dominique explained that Vannina was a sensitive young woman, perhaps too sensitive, who needed to be treated gently. She was trying to do her job better, but would never manage if she felt stressed, which was the case now. Would it be possible to show her more indulgence, even if she did make mistakes? Everything would work out for the best, he, Dominique, guaranteed it. He did not hear the vice-principal's answer. He saw the haughty expression, the disgust in the man's eyes, and caught only a few isolated words concerning his wife's stupidity and incompetence. Dominique muttered his excuses and left. He walked ten metres down the hall, then a great wave washed over him, blurring his vision. He wheeled around, went into the room without a word, and put the vice-principal's right hand beneath the blade of the paper-cutter. He wasn't talking anymore, he wasn't guaranteeing things would work out, all he wanted was to cut off the guy's hand as he screamed in terror and his body shook uncontrollably against his. The disgust he felt at the man's trembling body brought him back to his senses. He let him go and threw him against the wall. The vice-principal fell to the floor and covered his face with his hands. Dominique looked at him for a moment. "If my wife cries one more time, or even just looks sad, I'm coming back for you." He left the room, gasping for breath. He felt nauseous and weak. His victory filled him with horror. He felt no pride, quite the opposite, he bent beneath the weight of some basic form of shame, as if the indignity and weakness of his victim, a man like him, had contaminated him and sullied his very being. But Vannina never cried again. And he learned to live with the power that his strength conferred on him, the way the sage learns to live with the bitterness of truth.

He slammed his fist on the table. He shook his head, he refused to understand. "How can you justify it?" he kept asking Vincent.

"I am not justifying it," Vincent said. "I accept it."

"How can you accept it? How? I want you to explain it."

"It's not that I accept it, it's not about me, it's about sticking together. Personally, I would rather it hadn't happened. But it's done and we all have to live with it. Those dealers are dead and that's that."

"Those dealers? Explain it to me . . . Who were they? Mafia godfathers? Big-time criminals? International traffickers? They were . . ."

"No, Dumè, they weren't. I know as well as you do."

"No!" Dominique shouted. "They were no-good small-time hash dealers! And they're dead, God damn it! Did they deserve to die? Explain it to me! What horrible danger does their death protect us from? Tell me, God damn it! Tell me so I can understand!"

"Loads of people die who don't deserve to die, Dumè, people worth a lot more than them. In the Comoros, I saw loads of people who..."

"Forget that shit about the Comoros, Vincent! What are you talking about? Why are you telling me that people die? I know people die! I'm talking about people we kill, I'm talking about executions, and you're giving me shit with your abstract talk about death? Do you think..."

"Abstract, my ass!" Vincent finally started shouting too. "Don't tell me that what I saw was abstract, I saw women with dead babies in their arms, I saw more corpses than you'll ever see in your life! It's not abstract for me! You're busting my ass, and I'm going to save my tears and compassion for people who aren't shitty little dealers!"

"I can't believe you're saying that," Dominique said sadly, now that Vincent's sudden anger had calmed him down. "I can't believe it."

"It's your fault if I say stupid things," Vincent told him. "What happened is sad, alright. But we have to live with it. That's what I'm telling you."

"It's not sad, Vincent. It's shameful. I'll live with it. But it's shameful."

*

They were all at the bar to celebrate Stéphane getting out of prison. Virginie asked her mother if she could come and say hello to him along with everybody else, and when he walked in, glowing with happiness, she threw her arms around his neck and asked where he had been all this time. On vacation! In Brazil! At Club Med! Everyone had a different answer, and they laughed. Vincent and Dominique embraced him next. Drinks arrived from all quarters, the room began to spin, he was drunk on whisky, freedom and happiness, the lights turned circles and through the convivial fog he saw a militant from the local section, she had her eyes on him, she came closer and pressed against him, closer still until he felt her hot breath on his lips, and she said to him, come outside with me, come, right now, come!

(Finally, God, finally, someone listened!)

Not to be drunk. No. It's better, being drunk. There was frost on the windshield and it filtered the turning lights that followed Stéphane, the light from the stars perfectly round like in children's drawings, the streetlight, the light from his breath that glowed weakly in the darkness. It's better to be drunk to feel the girl's hot tongue on his lips, then down his shivering stomach, to hear her say, let me do everything, don't worry, I'll make you forget all that, let me do it, relax. (But I'm not worried, and I don't want to forget anything, I want to forget nothing of this blessing, this miracle that began with a pistol falling on the ground and ended with your mouth, finally, God, finally!) Stéphane leaned back against the seat, he turned his head left and right, slowly, because when he moved all the stars in the sky turned, the street-lights stood on their heads, all these wondrous lights gently transformed into distant halos by the frost, and so cold. He closed his eyes to touch the frozen windshield and feel the emptiness of his mind, the winter's biting cold, the burning mouth wrapped around him, the ecstasy and the embarrassment now, because what was happening was not what he had dreamed of for so long. (Not like that, God, not like that, don't do that to me, let me see you, let me touch you, let me learn and discover, not that way!) But he could not move. He opened his eyes. A few centimetres away, pressed against the glass, he saw Virginie's small desperate face, and her eyes watching him. (No, don't look at me, don't see me. Don't see me. I beg you.)

It is hard to know what Virginie actually saw. The cold had covered the car windows and windshield with white frost. How could anyone know what that spectacle represented for a little girl? Perhaps she witnessed it as a barbarous struggle whose meaning was mysterious, but that made her endlessly sad all the same. Maybe, for a moment, she was aware of the magnitude of the mystery she had come dangerously close to when she heard Stéphane cry from inside the car, "Stop! For God's sake, stop! The kid is there!"

He opened the car door.

"Are you alright, Virginie?"

"What are you doing here, you little brat?" the girl asked. "Don't you have anywhere else to be?"

"Shut up!" Stéphane told her. "Just shut up!" He got out of the car and squatted down next to Virginie. "Are you alright?" She looked at him and lowered her head as if she were about to cry. "No," Stéphane said, "don't cry, love, don't cry! Nothing's wrong. I don't want you to cry, I don't want you to be sad, ever, alright?" He smiled at her, then kissed her cheek. "Alright?" he said again. "Yes," Virginie answered. "O.K. Now, go back into the bar with your mother," he told her, trying to smile. "We'll see each other very soon. O.K.?" "Yes," Virginie said.

"We'll take the car and go somewhere else," Stéphane told the girl.

Stéphane drove a few kilometres. And he saw the girl the next day, in a bed where he could slake his thirst for contemplation. All knowledge is cruel, for it necessarily brings disillusionment. Mystical power was absent from the universe Stéphane was entering. That power belonged to the universe of things missing, of privation and fervour, and not to this one. Here were other things, interesting because they were unknown, but stripped of all sense of the sacred. In one way, it was a hundred times better than missing, but in another way, it was meaningless. His first experience turned him upside down, it was so extraordinarily great, so definitive, it went beyond anything he could explain. Overnight, and with the suddenness of a miracle, he lost all shyness and awkwardness, and the curse that had kept him from being noticed by women was lifted once and for all. In the space of a few months, at the university and in his region, he acquired the reputation of a ladies' man that made Tony Versini green with envy. But angelic purity was not to be found in that part of his life. When he showed up at the bar for weekend meetings, he always brought a little gift for Virginie. Marie-Angèle Susini considered him charming and thoughtful. She was delighted.

In 1988, the movement asked him to get involved with running the student union at Corte. He had proved his intellectual abilities and the time had come to entrust him with a major project. Stéphane had almost accepted being a brain. His involvement led him to study history from a new angle. He immersed himself in the archives with a passion, all this uncharted material waiting to be shaped into adequate form. He had the idea of publishing, at regular intervals and for the public face of the movement, a mimeographed series entitled *Our Memory*, which presented and analysed, in an academic format, the various events of Corsica's history that explained the legitimacy of the nationalist struggle. "History is there to be written," he told Vincent and Dominique. "It's not science – don't believe that. It's poetry and politics, you'll see." He wrote his monographs with a sovereign sentiment of power and exaltation. He felt like a great alchemist, a magnificent sorcerer exercising his craft directly in the labyrinths of memory to bring forth order and coherence. He took shapeless traces and transformed them into memory.

Stéphane was in a terrible mood. He had spent the previous night with a new girl, and he felt empty. It was late morning and he was alone in the bar. He ordered a coffee from Marie-Angèle. As soon as he finished it, nausea struck him. He was ripe for a migraine. He asked her for aspirin, but, ten minutes later, his headache had turned devastating. Marie-Angèle told him to lie down in the back room with the lights off. He followed her advice, pushing his clenched fists against his eyelids as he went, and found a spot where he could stretch out. He fought against convulsions for what seemed forever, caught between pain and intolerable nausea. Finally the aspirin began working its magic. He felt new life flooding back. He sighed in relief, but was careful not to open his eyes too precipitously. Then he heard someone at the door. The pain was leaving him more quickly now, and he felt pure blue sky fill his being. He opened his eyes. Virginie was standing next to him. He smiled at her. "I love you," she told him. "I'll always love you." She was as serious as the first time he had seen her, four years earlier. He had no answer. He could not joke or find some appropriate witty repartee, not because he was afraid to offend her, but because, inexplicably, he was convinced she was telling the truth. He breathed in deeply from within his immaculate sky. He heard the calm and profound beating of a heart he believed was his.

He thought of her. The nationalist movement was cracking on all sides under the weight of an enormously painful process of cell division, hatred oozing like bodily fluids, and he thought of her to retain some kind of purity. He participated with a sense of distance that saved him. His group was never threatened by a split, but the movement as a whole was. His life was intact. His activities unchanged. In Corte, half the students had stopped speaking to the other half. Stéphane could not care less. He continued looking after the union that was divided in two. In the winter of 1991, tensions were so high he bought a weapon, and Dominique and Vincent could not say a word about it – they even advised him to do as much. "Be careful," they said to him. "Especially in Corte. Here, there's no risk, you know that." He saw her on the weekends, and when he was not with her, he thought of her. When he went to bed with a girl and could barely tolerate her touch, he conjured up Virginie's serious face as a way to escape. She preserved him from hatred, migraines and disgust.

During the summer, as he was driving through the village, he saw her sitting on the wall by the fountain. He pulled up next to her and rolled down the window. She was sitting cross-legged. She smiled at him and closed her eyes. He looked at her, the top of her thighs. At the point where her skin turned so delicate it was almost transparent, her skimpy blue shorts revealed curls of pubic hair. Stéphane pictured the goddesses of the beaches, the nymphs of his former torments. He could not take his eyes off her. She kept hers closed. Her smile was dreamy.

"Virginie!"

He heard her name called.

He turned around. Ten metres away, Marie-Angèle's eyes were boring holes into both of them. He paid no attention. He was above it all. He heard the wild beating of his heart.

"My God, Virginie!" He did not recognise his own voice. "My God! It's over. You're not a little girl anymore."

She opened her eyes. Her smile left her face. The same serious, concentrated expression. Her long eyelashes. The same careful way of pronouncing her words. The truth.

"I never was a little girl."

A deep pulse darkened Stéphane's trembling soul. Could that really be my heart? he wondered.

"BEHIND YOU, THE SEA ..."

This is what our Uncle Hassan wrote:

My dear son, if such is your desire, I will gladly help you realise your project, with the help of God. I have made arrangements to send you the sum of fifteen thousand dirhams which should suffice for your passage. I am also ready to meet you in Algeciras but for me it is a long journey, I must be informed of your arrival far enough in advance to make the necessary arrangements. If I cannot come myself, I will find someone who can drive you safely to Marseille, and from there you may easily take a boat to Corsica. I spoke to my boss about you, and he has agreed to give you work as soon as you arrive. After, we will see how to find the papers you need for your status. The pay is good but you must understand that agricultural work is difficult and demands much stamina and strength of heart. I think you have considered that. As far as your desire to bring your younger sister with you, I am in complete disagreement, as, I am sure, your father would be as well. There is no work for women on the farm that employs me. What would she do? I can't think of anything she might be offered that would be proper for a girl, especially from the point of view of morals. And even if things were different, I could not pay for both your passages. Think about it, my son, and you will understand that the best thing for her is to live peacefully with her family, and wait to find a respectable husband. As for me, as I wait for the happiness of seeing you, I send you my blessing.

"You'll come anyway," Khaled said. "When he sees us both arrive, it will be too late to turn around. We too will have burned our ships. And I'll find the money, don't worry, I'll find it."

I know he'll find it. I also know I won't be able to say goodbye to anyone, and that hurts me. Two months later he told me he had enough money to pay my passage. He also managed to buy five hundred grams of hashish that we will take with us, and it will help us be free of care for a time in case we do not find work. He found out how much it can be sold for in France. And he said he understood why tourists take the risk of filling their cars with it before they leave Morocco.

One evening, we waited for them to go to bed and we left. We met the runner who was waiting for us on Playa Peligrosa.

You will write to them, you'll see, and when they understand how happy you are, they will forgive you and be as happy as you are. Don't be sad.

But I was sad.

Khaled gave half the money to the runner. He told him he would get the other half when we were in Spain. He didn't want to get cheated, and end up at dawn, alone and without a penny, on some other beach in Africa. The runner had to accept.

I was so sad as the boat slipped through the night. The sky was full of stars. We followed the coast as we travelled north. Khaled pointed out a fleeting light that the breaking dawn set dancing on the sea. Look, Hayet, it's the mark of a hoof. The night was ending, a single night. We went so far in so short a time. We gave the rest of the money to the runner. We were on a wide grey beach. I felt we were the only ones alive in the world. We came to a road and hitchhiked to Algeciras. When our uncle saw us arrive, both of us, he said nothing. Later, in the car, he asked one question: what will the girl do? Don't worry, Uncle, Khaled said. I will watch over her.

I was so sad as we drove. Along the roads, there were great bulls made of steel that cast enormous shadows on the hills. I felt the weight of all I had left behind. The familiar sounds of the medina. My mother. Our walks on Balco Atlantico, and most of all the ocean. I never saw it as a wall. My eyes do not see what Khaled's do. We went there for the last time two days ago. Boys were playing flamenco. Lovers were quarrelling. I looked as hard as I could, for the last time, at the sun sinking into the Atlantic. I don't understand why, but just then I knew that image would always torment me with nostalgia. I couldn't help myself, I was crying. Khaled took my hand. Don't be sad. My uncle looked at him and said nothing because there was nothing to say.

I was still sad in Marseille when we took the boat. The next day, in the rainy dawn, we saw from the bridge the great dark mass of the island breaking through the mist. I felt fear, not curiosity, as I discovered in the distance the land on which I would have to live. Our uncle said it was very beautiful. But under the low clouds, it only made my sadness harder to bear.

We drove some more. The road was narrow and twisting. We reached our uncle's house. There was a bed and a mattress on the floor. We'll find another mattress for her, he said. Tomorrow morning, you'll come to the vineyard with me.

No, Khaled said. Forgive me, Uncle, but I didn't leave Morocco to work in the vines. I will find something else. Something that will let me be closer to Hayet. Thank you for giving us shelter until then. I know we will find something very soon.

Our uncle shook his head, resigned.

May God give you protection, my son. God decides in the end. I can only give you what I have.

A week later, we left our uncle's house. Khaled had found work. He would be a dishwasher in a restaurant, and have a room there. And I met Marie-Angèle Susini.

MEMORY OVERLOAD

(1996–91)

My first memories of the hospital go back to when I was twelve, but they are vivid enough to keep me from forgetting that, inside such places, a person is treated like shit. When she returned home, my mother discovered me lying on my bed, howling in agony. She immediately took me to Trousseau, where a taciturn doctor undressed me, paying no mind to my childhood modesty, stuck a finger up my ass, and diagnosed a testicular torsion. Apparently, pulled by the weight of my left ball that was developing too rapidly, the cord on which it had hung, up until then, in a well-behaved fashion, twisted on itself, cutting off blood circulation. I required an emergency operation; without it, necrosis would set in within twenty-four hours. After they had shaved off the few pubic hairs that were a point of pride for me, I was taken to the operating room where the surgeon inserted a tube in my nostrils, stuck a fat, knobby finger up my ass again, God knows why, and allowed me to escape the shame of bursting into tears in front of everyone by anesthetising me. When I woke up, my hands were tied to the edges of the bed. My father was sitting next to me. His large nose twitched with concern and compassion. He called a nurse who came and untied me and warned me not to play with the stitches. Between my legs, completely filling my scrotum or almost, the guilty testicle had grown four times its normal volume, and I felt like crying again when I thought how for the rest of my life I might be forced to cart around an elephant ball that would turn me into an object of mockery and disgust. "The swelling will go down in no time!" my father tried to reassure me. But I could see he was in bad shape. My mother came in and immediately began to whimper and beg the Lord for mercy. "My poor Théo!" she blubbered. Both of them bent over me, their eyes wild. I felt ashamed of them. Of course, today I understand their worries. Fate had punished their only son, and in the nuts, to make matters worse. Through me, they expressed their anxieties about the future of their genetic material, fearing that the future cohort of theoretical descendants had been exterminated by the surgeon's knife, before I had even reached puberty. When the doctor showed up to examine me with all the care he would have given a heap of rotting meat (I remember keeping an uneasy eye on his finger and clenching my buttocks), my mother could not hold out any longer, and immediately demanded a guarantee of my fertility. My mother was certainly the most difficult and intolerable person I have ever been in contact with. Her unfailingly virtuous demeanour, her starchy good manners, and her little mouth shaped like a chicken's ass had no other purpose than to make her contemporaries feel guilty, starting with my father, by forcing them to behold the spectacle of her constant perfection. But I had to give her credit for one thing, she knew how to get what she wanted, and had enough contempt for the human race not to let herself be bossed around by the first consultant surgeon who happened to blunder into the room. This one had to set aside his gloomy persona and assure her there was no cause for concern. To reassure her completely, he pointed out that, even in case of further misfortune, one working testicle would be sufficient, in a future time reasonably distant, to make me the father of many children. "My baby boy!" she cried, suffocating me with her large breasts. No-one asked me if procreation was among my projects. True, I must not have had a clear idea of the subject, though even at that early stage I had no ambitions to reproduce. The idea that a person would be enthusiastic about bringing another human being into this world is something I could not imagine. Why would it be praiseworthy to extirpate from the void a being who had asked for nothing, and expose this person to sickness, suffering, taxes, and death – and would it not be natural justice if that same person paid back his genitors for their care by sending them to rot in an old folks' home once they had become a burden on him? I never quite understood it. When I shared my thoughts, one of my former colleagues and mistresses flew into a terrible rage. "And you call yourself an ethnographer, Théodore? You and your feelings of intellectual superiority! The groups we study don't see things that way, and they have a hundred times more reason to complain about their lot in life. But you have contempt for them, don't you? You think you're on a pedestal with your ten-cent cynicism! You're just a common piece of shit!" As I recall, that conversation put an end to our relationship. I didn't have time to tell her that the enthusiasm for giving birth that she ascribed to savage tribes did not constitute a valid argument in favour of reproduction. I was a cynic, or so it seemed. So what? I was ready to bring forth gods and jaguars but not human beings. Especially not ones who were anything like me.

So why is it that I got married and had children? It makes no sense. Unless the state of mind I am remembering, and the mistress who went with it, never truly existed. The whole problem lies therein. Incompatible memories, and no rational way to figure them out. On the one hand, logic offers us no hope of retracing a human life. So what does psychiatric medicine propose in order to help me? In my distress, after a series of catastrophes, in the autumn of 1994 I ended up going to see a psychiatrist and telling him everything, memory overload and ghost included. He proposed I be interned at Castelluccio. I agreed. I did not remember at the time how I had been treated at the children's hospital. I have memories that come at me from every which way, and for once, when they could have been useful, nothing appeared. I admit, I was drinking like a fish to get up the courage to tell all.

I signed the papers. It seemed like a good idea at the time. And that was how I found myself in Ajaccio, the very next day, completely lost in space, wearing pyjamas and a bathrobe, in front of Professor André Vincensini and Doctor Ghassan Fakhri. I had known better days. I tried to convince myself I had made the right decision, but could not believe in it anymore.

Vincensini was a fat pig with a smug air about him, around fifty years old, who had studied in Marseille, which was a very bad sign when you consider that a clan of Corsican mandarins had set up a system of back-scratching there, and that family ties, even of the most distant kind, worked better than competence and class attendance when it came to earning the sinister right to practise medicine. As for Fakhri, he was an Arab, enough said, in his thirties, with big dark eyes and long girlish eyelashes. I would rather not think about the quality of his education. I am no racist and I don't mind displaying compassion towards human suffering. But entrusting my health to the offspring of the Third World? That was a boundary I preferred not to cross. But no-one asked my opinion, it goes without saying. What was that guy doing in Ajaccio anyway? I bet no hospital worthy of the name had recruited him, and Vincensini was only too happy to find someone even more useless than he was, whom he could hire and tyrannise to his heart's content. They informed me I was to take some powerful medication to counter my hallucinations (without a word about the side effects on my libido) and, with Doctor Fakhri, engage in regular conversations that were exactly like psychotherapy – which seemed to me completely incoherent.

"Do you mind explaining?" I began. "Are we talking chemistry or the soul?"

Vincensini shrugged.

"Psychiatry is a pragmatic discipline, Mister Moracchini. We use any method that will help the patient."

"Do you think wearing pyjamas helps me? Why don't you give me my clothes back? I hate loungewear! I've always considered it ridiculous and degrading!"

My voice sounded terribly whiney, and brought to mind Gianfranco's tone, which I had not been able to rid myself of for weeks. I wanted to defend my dignity with more authority, but could not.

"You need to rest, Mister Moracchini," Fakhri said to me without answering my question.

He talked to me as if I were mentally deficient, or so it seemed, and his treacly, Levantine accent exasperated me. They left me alone. I was stuffed with tranquillisers and I believe I remember that, despite my distress, I quickly fell asleep.

At regular intervals, throughout my life, I have had recurrent dreams that fortunately I could not confuse with reality, and that left me no rest. There was the one where I saw Ruth and the children walking barefoot through the snow at Auschwitz, I knew they would not survive, and they went past me, glancing at me with terror in their eyes as I stood unmoving by the muddy road in an SS uniform. After I entered the hospital, I stopped seeing Gianfranco (assuming I had really seen him at one point and that he hadn't simply been, from the very beginning, like so many other things, part of memory overload), but I started dreaming about him. I was in a splendid house, full of light and benevolence, and I felt fulfilled. I had just rented it, I believe. Then, at the rear of the living room, I noticed an opening I had not seen at first. It gave onto a long, fussily decorated corridor that led in turn to other rooms that were heavily and magnificently furnished, bedrooms and boudoirs, bathrooms, an incredible number of rooms, but ever longer and narrower, ever darker and more dilapidated, weighed down with more and more knickknacks and wall hangings, with complicated spider webs here and there, dust and mould, then finally I came into a tiny room, completely filthy this time, and the little joy that remained was changed forever into anguish, then ecstasy as I laid eyes on Gianfranco, who was watching me from deep in the shadows with a smile both amiable and cruel. I awoke, laid low by nostalgia.

For much of my internment, I regretted ever having spoken of my problems. I did not know what Gianfranco was, a ghost, a hallucination, or memory overload. I often thought that made no difference – after all, real or imaginary, the objects of the world are, for us, never more than the content of our spirit, and I could have gone on living with him. I had never felt so alone. True, he was a complainer, a verbose, mannered spectre, as well as being a liar and a sadistic murderer, but I missed him all the same.

Fakhri asked me to tell him with as many details as possible what our relationship had been like. I explained that Gianfranco had appeared to me after I had moved to Corte, to a brand new dwelling that in no way corresponded to anyone's idea of a haunted house. He presented himself as a Corsican officer who had died a hero's death fighting the French troops in May of 1769. He very much enjoyed conjuring up the magnitude of his own heroism in a complex tale he had inflicted on me more than once. I grew accustomed to his presence, his chatty nature, the unpleasant aspects of his personality, so that, little by little, I ended up seeing only him, and even found something touching about him. But a week before I was interned, I met one of my historian colleagues who, horrified, showed me documents from the time which proved that Gianfranco was not a hero at all, but a monster who had delivered his village to the French army, participated in the systematic massacre of its population and raped several old women before personally slashing their throats. He was arrested as he tried to flee to Sardinia, but escaped hanging thanks to the people of the village where he was detained, who meted out justice themselves by lynching him with pitchforks and pickaxes.

I let Gianfranco know how betrayed I felt, and, after first trying to deny the truth, he inflicted the repugnant, dewy-eyed spectacle of his own chagrin upon me. I stood my ground, and he then had the nerve to accuse me of being as big a liar as he was, claiming that my ethnological treatises were no more than a tissue of fantastic inventions.

"So then," Fakhri said with that unshakeable and irritating air that moronic psychiatrists believe they have to display at all times, "you two share a common interest in hiding your motives and, if I understand correctly, this . . . phantom knew things you hadn't told anyone else. Is that it?"

"Alright, Ghassan, enough is enough, I can see what you're getting at, don't take me for a fool!"

"I am not taking you for a fool, as you say, and I will ask you to call me 'Doctor Fakhri' or 'sir', if you prefer," he said, trying to hide his vexation. "Now, please continue."

I told him again that discovering Gianfranco's crimes, even if they did scandalise me, had persuaded me momentarily that I was not suffering from hallucinations, but in fact was in the company of a ghost, one with doubtful morals, but real all the same.

"Momentarily?" he queried.

To my everlasting regret, I had to explain that, the next time I came across my historian colleague, he denied we had ever had the discussion I remembered with such perfect clarity. He did not understand what documents I was referring to, and had never heard the name Gianfranco de Lanfranchi. The shock was all the more terrible when, returning home and tormented by doubt, I turned to the notebooks in which I noted down most of the events of my existence, and in which I had carefully inscribed all my encounters with Gianfranco. Nowhere was his name mentioned. I recalled writing down the dates he appeared, and our subjects of conversation – but nowhere was his name mentioned.

I am not a cynic. I have been accused of being one, but that is simply not true. In one sense, I am the opposite of a cynic, for often the spectacle of this world devastates me. No doubt I have an excess of feeling, ineffectual, full of snivelling sensitivity, and that has never led me to change my ways or dedicate myself to the betterment of others, and my moments of distress are followed by long cold periods, I don't deny it, but this is a typical personal experience that does not seem compatible with cynicism. I am never stricken when there are great cataclysms or tragedies on a world scale, no, it always happens when I read some item in the paper, as if the world's misfortune appears in all its radical nature only through the tiniest viewpoint. I cut out two articles that cast me into temporary but profound depression during my stay in the hospital. The most recent dated back to 1996. In a dozen short lines, the local paper reported the murder of a homeless man from Poland: one of his companions, as drunk as he was, smashed in his skull with a bottle after a quarrel over how to divvy up the miserable pile of coins they had accumulated from begging. I imagined the Pole travelling south with a home-less person's dreams and ambitions that I could not even begin to describe. I burst into tears. The other occasion took place in 1994, shortly after I was hospitalised. The event occurred in a seaside town near my father's village. Two Arab dealers had been shot to death in the room they shared. They were employed as dishwashers in a restaurant. The article seemed to criticise the selling of hashish much more harshly than murder, and the tone was very moralistic. It had not occurred to the journalist that the dealer-dishwashers were not linked to high-flying inter-national traffickers. Up until then, I was alright. But there were photographs and names. One of the two was called Khaled, I believe. He was smiling at the camera. Behind him you could make out the sea or the ocean. They must have used a photo-graph taken during a vacation, or a family outing, in another life, who knows. But I remember finding that intolerable and I began crying with no hope of stopping, without knowing what – the photograph, the tone of the article, or the fact itself – had put me in such a state. Fakhri came into my room and found me, crying and blubbering, the newspaper in my hand. I really felt I was causing him pain. He came over to me and placed a hand on my shoulder (whose first effect was to make me blubber even more) and said, I promise things will get better, Théodore, we will take care of you, I swear. He might have been an incompetent doctor, but he acted with kindness, and, as I cried, I felt overcome with affection for him. The next day, when he returned, I greeted him with a big smile and warm salutations.

"Good to see you, Ghassan!"

"Doctor Fakhri," he said in a frosty voice.

I pointed out that the day before he had used my first name, which made me think our relationship had taken a new turn.

"Yesterday? I didn't see you yesterday."

I grew angry. I accused him of making shameful use of his knowledge of my problems to torture me, I told him I had noted down his visit and I was going to show him up immediately, and drag him before the college's disciplinary committee. In my notebook, dated yesterday, I found the newspaper articles, unpleasant reflections about the quality of the food and the physical appearance of the nurses – and no more. He had not lied to me. I had not seen him the previous day.

That is one of the painful aspects of memory overload, you approach the edge of infinity, and there is a real risk of losing yourself. What good is it to take notes if writing things down only adds to the lying memories? How could I reproduce every one of my actions and not turn into the distant reflection of a reflection? I set myself a rigorous, disciplined regime. Every morning, I reread the notes I had made the day before. I did not mention our discussions to Fakhri or anyone else unless I had first made sure they had truly taken place. As for the more distant past, though in the end it made little difference whether it was real or not, since it existed, no doubt, in my memory only, I took no precautions and avoided wondering about it whenever possible. But it was not easy making those resolutions. I was fond of my past. More so than of my image or my health. At times I revolted, especially in the weeks before my internment, and afterwards there were sporadic violent episodes at the hospital, and Fakhri was the butt of those.

When my historian colleague denied ever having spoken to me about Gianfranco, I remained convinced, even after realising I had taken no notes about him, that he was lying to me for a reason I would need to discover. I launched a discreet investigation involving Stéphane Campana. I had been seeing him on a regular basis ever since he had sought me out for conversation shortly after I came to Corte in 1991. Since I knew he was looking after one of the two nationalist student unions, I feared at first that he would spew the party line and make absurd demands concerning God knows what. In Corte more than anywhere else, making demands enjoyed a special status in itself, and no-one was concerned with the nature of the demand. But I was wrong. To my office came a handsome young man, extremely courteous and sympathetic, who thanked me for agreeing to see him. He asked me if I had had the chance to read one of the pamphlets entitled *Our Memory* that were circulating around the university.

I had read two of them. One of them covered the rebellion against conscription and the troubles that followed in the 1820s in Fiumorbu, and the other the military expedition that eradicated banditry in 1932. The pieces were well-argued, well-researched, well-written, and presented in an academic format, with footnotes and bibliography, though this apparent concern with objectivity served only to disguise the ferociously partisan intention whose sole goal was to justify nationalism and prove the existence of the nation through time, the glory of its martyrs, and other similar nonsense.

"You mean those propaganda pieces?" I asked him.

He laughed openly.

"That's right, sir," he agreed. "Those propaganda pieces. I write them."

I told him I was sorry, I had no intention of offending him. But he was not offended. He knew very well what he was doing. He was ready to admit that historical objectivity was not his problem, and such objectivity, even if you argued that theoretically it could exist, was completely impossible once the meaning of the past became part of the political struggles of the present.

"In other words," I said to him, "your interest is not history, but politics."

"I have never completely understood the difference," he confessed. "And you can't tell me I'm the only one, even if others don't express it in such clear terms."

What a charming young man when I think about it! I could not tell him as much, but he reminded me of myself when I was a youth, though with greater honesty. All that pontificating crap I listened to about the scientific veracity of the social sciences! Of course I never believed in any of that. Which was why falsifying sources and fantastic interpretations never frightened me. We want to write a good novel, coherent and well thought out, about culture, or the past, and that's that. The novel Stéphane dreamed of was a bloody epic, full of nobility and death rattles. I appreciated quieter stories. Fine. Nothing remained of them, in any case. No use lamenting that.

"And how can I help you, friend?" I asked him, all smiles.

"I'm about to start writing my history thesis about violence in Corsica since the seventeenth century. There are a lot of interesting things to say."

"You must know by now that I am an ethnologist, not a historian."

He explained it would be impossible to do the research he wished to without solid ethnological references, notably those concerning family structures and the settling of conflicts in the absence of State authority, he was a novice in the area and was in absolute need of my help. He added, if I remember rightly (and if it is not true, it is still a pleasant memory), that he loved my work, that his thesis director was an asshole (which was the utter truth), and that it would be an honour to benefit from my knowledge.

I have never been insensitive to flattery, that is a fact, and I found him increasingly likeable. I agreed to answer his questions. We began to see each other on a regular basis and our relationship was, at the time, most cordial and honest (of course I could not admit to the liberties with reality I had taken in the works that had made such a vivid impression on him). Vendettas fascinated him, he spent long periods of time in the archives, and had an impressive storehouse of horrible anecdotes that he took great delight in sharing with me and that I helped him place in their supposed cultural context. I decided to tell him, though I remained wary, about Gianfranco and the suspicions I had about my historian colleague.

He had never heard of a traitor who had betrayed his village to the French military, which caused me great pain. If such a traitor had existed, I asked him, would there be something to gain from concealing his existence? That seemed possible, desirable, even. The traitor I described would have no place in the tragic yet honourable tableau of this small but virtuous nation subjugated by the large and greedy nation, and the best thing was to act as though he had never existed. He did not doubt that such traitors had well and truly existed, even if he had no knowledge of them. The fact they had been forgotten seemed to him a healthy sign.

"Memory must be selective, Mister Moracchini," he told me, "otherwise we expose ourselves to painful disorders. I believe what I am saying is true for nations as well as individuals."

Little did he know the truth of what he said. For a time he comforted me with the certainty that the bastard of a historian, frightened by the trust he had placed in me, now claimed he had said nothing, and that memory overload had nothing to do with it. Unfortunately I could not hang onto that idea for long. I believed in it, then I stopped believing in it. Nothing was stable. And I was exhausted. Gianfranco was now appearing only sporadically. He was grumpy, he sulked, and he had stopped talking to me. I even lost my taste for fucking. After completely going off the rails during a reception organised by the university president to which the entire body of professors and student representatives had been invited, and during which everyone exchanged concerned looks with one other, I entered a short period of peacefulness. I confessed to my deceptions with a certain panache; no-one would make me associate with people who had lied to me, or might not even exist. I intended to stay safe behind locked doors, seek reconciliation with Gianfranco, and not put my nose outside. But two days after the reception, the telephone rang. It was the secretary of the department asking me why I had not given my Master's seminar. The students were waiting for me. I slammed the receiver down. Then took another look at my notebooks for the day of the reception. Nothing. I thought I might have written on a loose sheet, and turned the house upside down looking for it. Nothing. I picked up the telephone again and asked the psychiatrist to see me immediately. All around, scattered in every direction, were the dozens of pairs of ladies' underwear covered in scribbling. My life's work.

As I said, I did have moments of rebellion in Castelluccio. When that occurred, my aggression would pour out on Fakhri, whom I found terribly antipathetic at the time, to the point that I could not tolerate him. Especially when he tried to make me talk about my parents.

"My mother was a domestic tyrant, an Oedipal nightmare, and my father had no balls. And that's why I see ghosts – there, I just saved you a lot of time. I don't see how one thing explains the other."

My father, my mother, my childhood! What else would you expect to find in a childhood other than distress and anxiety? What's the point? I told him to leave my childhood alone. He wanted me to talk about my wife and children. I refused. One day I told him I was certainly not going to talk about my wife, who had the misfortune of being Jewish, to a pro-Palestinian Muslim so he could accuse her of all the evils on earth.

"I don't know why I would attack a woman who might not even exist. Besides, I'm Lebanese and a Maronite Christian, Mister Moracchini."

"Don't play word games with me, Fakhri!"

"It's *Doctor* Fakhri. You know, Mister Moracchini, I have a hard time believing you were a renowned ethnologist. To me you seem seriously racist."

When I saw he was having trouble controlling himself, I enjoyed a deep satisfaction. Today, I am much less proud. A few days later, he returned to see me in the company of a young woman wearing glasses and a frightened expression, whose eyes darted here and there. She was a psychology student serving an internship. She cast her worried eyes upon me. I was unshaven, in pyjamas, drugged to the eyeballs, and I scared her. The magic of the psychiatric hospital at work, I suppose. And I was hopping mad. I imagined they had come in hopes of hearing the complete catalogue of my symptoms. They sat down in front of me. I told Fakhri I had made a full public confession at the university, but everyone acted as though nothing had happened.

"What would be the point of that?" Fakhri asked me.

"To keep me on as professor. I was the only professor of renown in that second-rate university, and they didn't want to lose me."

"What about the ghost? A ghost that has so many interesting points in common with yourself?"

"Gianfranco is sadly real," I said. "And my historian colleague is a liar. I'm sure he destroyed all the documents concerning him."

"But he hasn't appeared since you've been here. Since you've been under our care, is that not true?"

"That's because he can appear only in my house in Corte,

or maybe your medication stole my possibility of seeing him, though he is truly there ... How should I know?"

"So, to summarise, contrary to what you have admitted over the last weeks, you have supernatural gifts and, in addition to that, you are the victim of a plot, is that it?"

"Yes, I'm the victim of a plot, and I do have gifts!" I shouted – and immediately realised the disastrous effect of my declaration.

The lady student swallowed carefully. I let my anger flow. No more whining!

"It's easy to present things that way, and make a mockery of people. If I were born in Siberia and the same thing happened to me, I would be a shaman, understand, and I would be respected, and I wouldn't have to justify myself to someone like you, who ridicules everything I say. Have you considered that?"

"So, you are not sick, is that it?"

"Yes, I am sick!" I howled, and started to cry. "But not the way you think! You are a bad doctor, you are incompetent, you understand nothing about my sickness!"

"Let's go," Fakhri said to his intern, who did not have to be asked twice.

As they moved towards the door, I went on shouting and crying.

"It's too easy! What the hell did you come here for in the first place? Isn't there anyone to cure in your own country? But that frightened you, I bet, you prefer more civilised kinds of mental disorder, young ladies' neuroses, comfortable Western psychoses. Real problems like war, you're too much of a coward!"

He stopped and I could see I had hit the mark. In the hallway, the student asked him what diagnosis he had for me. "Diagnosis?" he shouted, beside himself. "He's a schizophrenic, a completely decompensated paranoid schizophrenic!" Then he flung open the door and stuck his head into my room. "Not to mention being a son-of-a-bitch!" he yelled before slamming the door as hard as he could.

The next day, Vincensini honoured me with a visit. He told me straightaway that nothing compelled him to keep me here, and that if my attitude towards Doctor Fakhri did not change, they would put me out on the street and I could go set up shop in Siberia. Was that my choice? No, I answered pitifully. Vincensini informed me that Fakhri no longer wished to have me as his patient. I asked Vincensini to bring him in, if only for a minute. When he entered my room, I realised again how much I had hurt his feelings the previous day. He looked even younger than usual.

"I'm sorry," I said. "Honestly, I'm sorry."

He nodded. "That's alright. Think nothing of it."

I began to cry again. I was at the end of my tether. I wasn't just whimpering; my pain was beyond naming. Like with the newspapers. The fact that he accepted my apology shook me, no doubt. Not to mention the medication. Finally I heard my voice, the words I was babbling as I cried. "My little girl . . . My little girl . . ."

Fakhri must have heard those words too. He came closer and placed his hand on the back of my neck. "It's alright, Théodore, we'll take care of you, you'll see. I made a mistake yesterday. My job is to understand. Everything will be fine." That was the end of my revolt. The next morning, I hurried to read my notebook. The words that Ghassan Fakhri had spoken were written there, clear as day, next to Sarah's name.

When I left my house in Corte for the last time, before going to Castelluccio with my notebooks and collection of panties, I heard Gianfranco's voice telling me he had forgiven me, I must not leave him, if I did I would regret it. He said he was the only friend I had. And that I was the only friend he had ever had. But I turned the key in the lock and got into my car. It was too late. I was ready to leave him behind. Life is not coherent, don't try and tell me it is. I tried to trace a line from the charming young man from Corte, the haughty and scornful guy I met in the village, and the poor, shattered corpse that lay in front of Marie-Angèle's house. I never succeeded. I tried to understand what, in my person, could have attracted Marie-Angèle's attention, and I did not succeed in that either. Yet these things are real. We may not understand them; that changes nothing. What would keep me from believing I had abandoned what I loved most in the world, and that I did it in an atmosphere of carefree joy, and now I could not live with what I had done? What would keep me from believing that I was mourning a girl who was very real, I who had never wanted children? And if nothing kept me from believing those things, no-one could say it wasn't true. No-one had the right to make that claim. So, in a way, I was ready. I put my affairs in order. My suitcases full of notebooks. The panties. I folded my pyjamas and put on the suit I would wear for my arrival. I looked around the room. The newspapers I had accumulated over the last two years, with their columns of obituaries. I was still among the living. Ghassan walked me to the front of the hospital. It was a beautiful day. The air smelled not of medication, but of cistus and fresh air. I said I intended to live in my father's house, in the village. Ghassan nodded.

"It will be alright," I said.

"Of course it'll be alright, I don't doubt it."

He shook my hand. Then gave me a warm hug. He said something in Arabic with a smile. I asked him what it meant.

"May God bless you," he replied.

"You don't really believe in psychiatric medicine, do you?" I said, laughing.

"Take your medication anyway, just in case."

I turned and left. He was waving goodbye and smiling. I left him behind as well, I let him fade and gently turn into a memory, the way we all do. First memories, then nothing.

"BEHIND YOU, THE SEA ..."

Every day, during my break, I go down to see Khaled in the town. I always find someone to drive me. He is happy. The owner of the restaurant gave him a room that he is sharing with Ryad, an Algerian he works with in the kitchen. They get along well. At first Khaled was a little worried. Ryad woke him up at five o'clock in the morning with his prayers. You do all five prayers? Khaled asked him. Are we going to have this racket every morning? Ryad reassured him. He would try and make less noise, and in any case, it wasn't going to last long. It was a promise in memory of his father. He swore that, if ever he managed to leave Algeria, for a month he would behave like a perfect Muslim. The month will be over in three days. I was afraid, Khaled said. Ryad started to laugh. If you like, in three days we'll go get a beer. I will become a sinner again. Khaled agreed.

He wanted to show me his room. There are two beds with green wool blankets, and at the rear, not even hidden by a curtain, Turkish toilets with a shower head above them. The wind blows through the place. Khaled says it doesn't matter. Nothing matters since we came here. He says it's better than back home. In a way it's true, but back home, at least, the toilet had a door. He said it's not important. And he was happy when I said I have a nice room with a toilet just above the bar. He asked if everyone was acting polite with me. I told him Marie-Angèle is a good woman, she has a little girl, and the men who come to the bar, the regular customers, are very nice and would never let anyone harm me. I'll come and see you some day, Khaled told me.

No, I don't think so. And you know why.

Of course he knows. He didn't need long to find out. In the whole town, there is only one bar where Arabs go. And it's not because they want to be together. No-one has tried to go anywhere else. No-one has wanted to. Here too, there are invisible walls. It's easier for me because I'm a girl. I can almost forget. But he can't and I'm afraid his good mood won't last. Of the two of us, he is the more fragile, even if he doesn't know it.

That day we had tea with Ryad. I don't know him, but he is very nice. He wanted us to tell him about our city. I told him there is a long promenade running along the ocean, and it's very nice to stroll there, it's called Balco Atlantico. From there, I told him, you can see the most beautiful sunsets in the world.

Ryad's father died in an attack on the rue Didouche-Mourad in Algiers. A bomb exploded as he was walking by. Life became impossible. In Blida, one of his aunts found three heads on the pavement when she stepped outside. The day after his father was buried, the imam came to his house to read from the Qur'an. His mother requested it. To hear the word of God comforts her. The living room was full of neighbours and friends. First the imam read Al-Fatiha and the Surah of daybreak. He read very well. Then he wanted to say a few words. We must not mourn the death of believers, for what we call death is what true life is. We must learn to separate ourselves from earthly existence as soon as possible. This existence, for the one who knows, is contemptible and worthless compared to the eternal beatitude of the soul, promised to all those who believe that there is no god but God and that Mohammed is His prophet. Ryad's mother stood up, she was trembling. You are a terrorist. Maybe you don't have blood on your hands, but the one who glorifies death the way you do is a terrorist. I believe in paradise and I mourn my husband with no shame, before you and before God. But you, you sully the name of the Prophet with your words. Didn't He love women? Didn't He love life? May God forgive you, but in the meantime, leave my house. I don't want terrorists under my roof. That evening, his mother told Ryad he had to find a way to get out of Algeria as quickly as possible. Save yourself. There is nothing good in this country, nothing at all. Just the impious love of death. Go and live. Somewhere else. Remember how the Prophet loved life. And that was when Ryad made his promise.

We didn't know what to say. My shift was starting soon and I had to find a way to get back to the village. In town, I met Vincent Leandri who agreed to drive me back. He asked me if I liked it here. I said yes. Then he said that if I ever had any problems, even a small one, I could count on him. I thanked him. He told me I was beautiful again, then nothing more. A minute later he added that that wasn't why I could count on him.

A few days later, Khaled had a present for me. Earrings. He also bought a watch for our Uncle Hassan. He was very proud to be able to give me a gift. He told me he had started selling our hashish. When people found out he had brought it directly from Morocco, he was swamped with requests. In a few days, he won't have any left. But that doesn't matter, he didn't come here to sell hashish. He's making a living, he doesn't need it. With half the money he makes, he will buy me clothes and other little presents. The other half he will send to our parents.

Khaled, that's not right, you should send everything to them.

No, not everything. I don't want to. You should have a better life too.

A YOUNG GIRL'S DREAM

(1991–96)

"No, don't look at me! I can look, but you can't!"

Lying naked on her bed, Virginie closed her eyes, she closed them docilely and fervently. She obeyed Stéphane's voice and did not move as if, all that time, she was listening to her own marvelling voice that spoke in the silence of her soul. He was sitting on a chair facing her. He was looking at her, it went on forever. He would rather die than touch her. But he felt no shame at being in her room this way. He cared nothing for Marie-Angèle's disapproval. There was no reason for shame or embarrassment in what he was doing. With Virginie he soared far above the ordinary criteria of moral judgment, in the ethereal atmosphere of the constant intoxication of the spirit. On the wall by the fountain, Virginie suddenly became feminine without ceasing to be an angel. It was absolutely inexplicable. When she told him again that she loved him, he had to yield to the force of truth and answer that he loved her too. For he did love her. But how? What did that mean? He wanted to feel her closeness, he wanted to see her and take pleasure in her beauty, but without profaning anything. When she asked him the first time if she could take her clothes off, he accepted immediately, no hesitation, no blushing. He opened his eyes and saw her watching him in his contemplation. In this game of reflections, he felt there was something evil he must avoid at all costs. He asked her to close her eyes. He would go on asking her for months. Though she did have the right to speak.

"Will you make love with me?" she asked.

"Yes, but not right away. In a few years."

"But when? I'm ready now. When?"

"In a few years. Not long."

"But you said you loved me."

"Yes. And that's why. Because I do love you."

He was so sincere. Virginie closed her eyes and seemed to believe him. As Stéphane's gaze travelled across her body and made her shiver, perhaps she was imagining the first time they would make love. The first time he would ask her to open her eyes. After gazing at her for what seemed like forever, he asked her to get dressed. When she did, he took her in his arms and held her as tightly as he could, breathing in her perfume and placing kisses on her forehead.

The year went by slowly, and Vincent felt more tired, and more nostalgic. The split in the ranks was exhausting him. Leaning on the bar, he smiled benevolently at Hayet, the new waitress Marie-Angèle had hired. Her beauty was perfect but her melancholy, more visible than her beauty, moved him. He loved waitresses. In each of their faces, he saw the traces of unhappy love, something poignant he dreamed of and, in his romanticism, hoped one day they would confide in him. He loved to look at them and speak with fraternal compassion. Better that than the palpable hatred he could not get rid of since the split. Vincent could not believe he could feel such radical hatred towards men he had considered brothers for years. He realised his hatred went beyond personal disputes, or even concrete ones. He hated them as a group, solely because they had separated and were no longer on the same side he was. Vincent was much too intelligent to be satisfied with that motive but, to his surprise, his hate remained just as intense. He wondered if it were no more real than his former feelings of fraternity.

He ended up confiding in Dominique. The latter was categorical.

"You hate them because they're hateful. The best they deserve from us is our contempt. I won't even take the trouble to hate them. All I want is for them to stay away. They screwed up fifteen years of struggle."

Vincent had his doubts.

"They must think the same about us."

"Because they're mistaken. You're not sure you're right?"

"Yes, I'm sure. But my problem is that I don't know why I'm so sure. I'm not trying to let them off the hook or anything, you know what I think about them. But that's what doesn't seem clear to me."

Dominique shrugged. Vincent envied him a little. In him he detected a luminous, unshakable conviction that he himself, he knew too well, did not possess. Dominique believed that Good and Evil were always clearly identifiable. And he was no fool, not by any means. His heart was pure. To keep his world from turning to ash, he had to think that the options chosen by the others were evil, as were the motives that had pushed them to make their choices. It was that simple. And yet, Vincent would have sworn, he suffered terribly from the split. It shook the very foundations of his life. But the certainty of being on the right side helped him withstand the pain. Vincent could not see things the same way. He did not think it was a matter of convictions or political options. There was something profound and bestial there, like the unleashed violence of the pack instinct, a savage desire to assert one's own life against the rest. From deep in his animal memory came the war cry that rallied men, the joyful howling of excited beasts, the panicked lament of the prey, the feasts of blood. Hatred is joy, when it comes down to it, full of vitality. Lovers do not regret their lost unity. They pray for war. In the uproar of the wars to come, Vincent stopped hearing the beating of his sombre heart and the waves of sadness he had never stopped fighting against.

*

Lines were being drawn. The familiar physiognomy of the world was abruptly transformed by the enmity of men. There were any number of places, streets, cafés, restaurants, entire villages where they could not go because the others were in the majority. It was like they had been wiped off the map. An invisible iron curtain ran through Corte and the atmosphere there was particularly heavy. Each side had its strongholds in their respective bars, but students from the two sides could not help crossing paths on the Cours Paoli or in the same amphitheatre. The bill-posters and the pamphlet-pushers from the two enemy unions often came face to face. Fights followed by death threats broke out from time to time. Old friendships were reduced to bitterness. The tension was constant. But the situation had not degenerated completely. Every time Stéphane had to go to the university, Virginie was sick with worry. She begged him to stay with her. When he refused, as he did every time, explaining kindly that he simply had to go, she began to cry, which did not keep her from gazing at him with admiring eyes, as if he were exhibiting superhuman courage. She begged him, at least be careful, never go out without your weapon. He lacked the honesty to tell her she was exaggerating. He liked being admired, though he did not feel admirable. Dominique and Vincent continued to use him for his intellectual qualities alone. His illegal activities were limited to regular participation in the clandestine press conferences that were very frequent at the time. Wearing a black jumpsuit and a wool balaclava that made his skin itch, he stood standing, unmoving, a pump-action rifle in his hand, next to other militants dressed as he was while, at a makeshift table covered with a Moor's-head flag, a pseudo spokesman (an entry-level militant chosen for his perfectly unremarkable voice) read a text to a selected audience of journalists who had been escorted out into the backcountry. It was not a particularly exalting ritual. The next day, when Stéphane recognised himself in the newspaper photograph, he thought he looked like an ass. No style at all. Still, he cut out the picture and gave it to Virginie. She cried out in childish wonder and threw her arms around his neck. Then she went and lay down naked on the bed, making extra sure not to open her eyes. How could he tell her he was being treated like a pawn? He would let her think what she wanted. But he did not lie to her. He had thought from the beginning that since he could not give her the loving embrace she was waiting for, he owed her something greater and rarer: the truth. He hid none of his activities from her. If his comrades had criticised his lack of caution, he would not have understood. Caution would have been insulting to her, it was inconceivable. From the things he told her, Virginie built a temple to his glory. Stéphane was flattered and embarrassed. He wished his comrades would let him demonstrate that he did deserve a little of her fervent admiration. Going every week to Corte, wasn't that an act that demanded courage? Perhaps, but he did not see it that way. All this agitation was fictitious, he felt, and deep down, no-one took it seriously and no-one truly feared it. It seemed to him more important to continue writing his articles. He had begun a doctoral thesis on the history of violence and asked Professor Théodore Moracchini for his help. He had recently arrived in Corte and agreed to give him important ethnological information and the advice on methodology that he needed. Their meetings occurred on a regular basis and went remarkably well. Stéphane had no academic ambitions. He did not picture his life anywhere else than with the movement. But he wanted to satisfy his intellectual aspirations and orient them towards reconstructing a past everyone could be proud of. When he could take time off from running the union, he went to study in the archives. He forgot the threats of the present by diving into the dark family conflicts of the past. He returned with terrible stories of revenge and murder, stories of unspeakable brutality, and recounted them to Virginie in her dreamy beatitude.

One night in Corte, after a meeting, he ended up in a girl's room. For the two years he had been with Virginie, he had had no sex life. The only nudity he laid eyes on belonged to a teenage saint. His only ecstasy was spiritual. That night, his pleasure was unforgettable. And come morning, guilt and a migraine awoke him in a bed in a university dorm. The girl's naked body repulsed him. He got up and left as soon as he could. His head was a mass of suffering, and his nausea refused to subside. In his mind, the punishment was well-deserved. Virginie was waiting for him in the village. When he arrived, she saw by his grey face that he had been in pain all that day, as he often was, and she placed her cool palms on his forehead to soothe him. He never lied to her, he never hid anything from her. He told her he had slept with a girl. She turned so pale he was afraid she would die, and that he would die with her. Love and compassion tore him in two. He talked to her endlessly, holding her close, he told her it didn't matter, it didn't mean anything, he had been tricked by the needs of his body, so make love with me, Virginie said, I'm fifteen now, but he told her no, he said it was impossible, she was still too young and he didn't want to dishonour her, he said she was full of illusions, it wasn't as beautiful as she thought it was, even when you love someone as much as he loved her, there was always something dirty about it. Because you love me, you still love me? Virginie asked in a supplicant's voice, and he felt the poison of love flow through his burning veins. I love you more than anything. I don't even know how to say it. I'd die if you were unhappy. Yes, Virginie said, yes. I know you love me.

The next week in Corte, he went to bed with another girl, then another. The guilt turned into something vague, almost unreal. It was true: it did not count. It bore no relation to the grandeur of his love. Nothing was taken away from Virginie. Nothing could be. I love you, I'm not stealing anything, no-one can take anything from you, the things that belong to you are so great the others don't even know they exist, they're beyond what they can dream of, you must believe me, you don't need to cry, you're breaking my heart, they don't know it exists and you have it, it's yours, listen to me, look at me, look at me and see whether I'm lying, have I ever lied to you? Never, Virginie said, wiping away her tears. Those girls don't matter at all, they're so meaningless I'm not hiding them from you, other people lie to each other, the other guys all lie to the woman they love, but I don't lie to you, I will never lie to you, and that's important, you own the truth, it belongs to you, you have to understand, the body has its needs, you can't just ignore them, but it doesn't matter, are you jealous when I eat? Jealous of the food? No, Virginie said. Well, it's the same thing, believe me, exactly the same. But are we going to make love? Yes, when you're eighteen, we'll make love, in three years, for you and me three years is nothing, and when we make love, I'll never make love to anyone else but you. I swear.

Hayet was beginning to look prettier and prettier to Tony Versini. At the same time, she was teasing him in a way he could not understand.

"She's playing games," he said. "I'm telling you, she's playing games with me."

"I don't think so," Vincent told him. "I really don't think so. First, she is very, very beautiful, and that always makes a woman look a little haughty, and then, besides that, she's sad. So little assholes like you who don't know anything about sadness and even less about beauty think she's playing games."

Everyone laughed but Tony would not let up. Hayet was playing games with him.

"What's worse," Stéphane added, "is that you think you're so irresistible, and that any girl who doesn't fall into your arms must be playing games with you. Maybe you think you're God's gift to women, but she doesn't share your opinion. If you want that girl, you'll have to make an effort. And you don't even know what that means, making an effort. All you're good for is fucking whores."

"Anyway," Tony said, "whores or not, I can't fuck an Arab girl."

"Wait a minute," Vincent said, "didn't you just say she was very attractive?"

"Yes," Tony said.

"And very beautiful?"

"Yes."

"So what's with all this bullshit?"

Tony tried to explain. The point wasn't whether a girl was beautiful or not, or whether he liked her, he just couldn't fuck an Arab girl, or a black girl either, but he wasn't racist, he could fuck a Chinese girl if he needed to, it was a physical thing, it was impossible. There was something unhealthy about it. Besides, Arab girls had strange habits according to what he knew, like shaving their pussy and taking it up the ass at a moment's notice.

"Where did you get that shit?" Vincent asked in disbelief. "Have you been studying it? And anyway, even if it was true, no-one's asking you to take it up the ass, and what have you got against shaved pussies?"

"Nothing," Tony admitted.

"Then what's the problem?"

"I just don't think I could fuck an Arab girl."

Vincent looked at him with a combination of disgust and terrible affection, as if he were a retarded baby brother. He gave his ear a pull.

"You really are the king of assholes, Tony. I hope you know that!"

Each time, he would slump back on the chair facing the bed where Virginie's naked body lay. To spare her the effort of having to keep her eyes shut, he bought her a black silk blindfold she could keep tied around her head as he gazed at her. He had resumed an active sex life and the memory of the many female bodies sullied Virginie and infected her like gangrene. Hers was still the body of an angel incarnate, but tiny shadows, like growths of mould, began to appear. Her belly was pale and divine, but her pubic bush was an organic stain. He asked her to shave it. Do you love me? Virginie murmured in the isolation of her darkness. Yes, I love you. He looked at the nail of her little toe, the nail was a tiny bit twisted, and at the toes themselves and the shape of her feet, and it seemed that her extremities were less suited to the saintliness of an angelic body. He asked her to keep her feet covered. She stopped taking off her shoes. But her ankle, perfectly round with its delicate blue veins, her ankle was saintly. She put on socks. The gangrene spread and its nature changed. At the same time the imperfections of Virginie's body filled him with terrible sexual potency that issued from her like steamy, toxic sweat, and, on his chair, Stéphane could not turn away from the current of excitement that engulfed and horrified him, the excitement was monstrous, no known act could appease it. The world turned inside out like a glove. The sky was a terrifying abyss. Something enormous had taken place while Stéphane was sitting on his chair, unaware. Now it was too late. He had to resign himself. First he struggled and resisted, but it was no use, resigning himself was not enough, he had to desire what was taking place, want it with all his strength, answer yes when over and over Virginie asked him, do you love me? Answer yes, more than ever, tell her too that the meaning of love had changed, what was once great was now out of all proportion, unnamable, too big for the human mind and its laws. Stéphane left his chair. They did not make love. What they did awaited a name. Virginie heard him orbit around her and moan like a man possessed. She smiled and moaned too, alone in her darkness, but so united with him that she knew how his blood tasted, the texture of his wounded flesh, the bitterness of his desire. She cried, do you love me?

And he answered yes, his voice unrecognisable, and downstairs, Marie-Angèle covered her ears and dreamed of Stéphane's death. Then, like the other times, he held Virginie close with the purest tenderness, an embrace of heavenly chastity, he kissed her forehead, and later, in the shower, she would let the hot water wash away the dross that lay upon her like the dead skin of a snake and she would be pure once more, but he embraced her as if she were already pure, and as he held her this way he told her, one evening in 1994, that the next day he was going to kill a man.

"What the hell are you doing, you dirty whore, you shitty little Arab?"

Hayet slapped Tony hard in the face but no-one had seen what led to it. Now he completely lost it, he was insulting and grabbing her. Vincent did not think twice. He took hold of Tony and threw him against the wall. He stood between him and Hayet and raised his fist. But Tony's anger was already draining away. He lowered his head. Marie-Angèle started berating him and he did not try to defend himself. He turned to Hayet and said he was sorry. That did nothing to calm Marie-Angèle's anger.

"He understood," Vincent said. "I promise you he understood."

Hayet wanted to go back to her spot behind the bar.

"You can go home, love," Marie-Angèle told her. "You've been through enough for one night."

Tony had had too much to drink. He forgot his principles when it came to Arab women, and started coming on strong to Hayet. Drunk as he was, and used to hanging out with tourist girls who were always ready for a little action, his come-on was a little too strong, and Hayet slapped him to make him see the light. Tony was completely sober now, and he could not meet anyone's eye. Vincent had saved him from the full force of Marie-Angèle's wrath. He went over to Tony and made him look him in the face.

"You're an asshole, a double asshole. First because you're hassling that girl who never did anything to you, and then because you can't control yourself in Marie-Angèle's place. What kind of example is that? You got a problem with your nerves? You don't like getting slapped? Now you listen to me. The next time you do something like that, I'll show you what it's like to get slapped for real. Understand? I'll beat you to within an inch of your life!"

Tony nodded. Then it was Dominique's turn.

"And when Vincent is through with you, I'll take over. Now go home and sleep it off, go back to town, we've seen enough of you."

The next afternoon, when he went to buy cigarettes in the port, Tony was approached by an Arab man he had never seen who wanted to talk to him. "I've got nothing to say to you," Tony told him, "get lost." The Arab headbutted him and Tony ended up on the ground. He tried to pull his pistol from his belt but the Arab stomped on his hand, leaned over, took the gun and threw it away, then kicked him in the ribs so fast and so hard he did not understand what was happening to him. Tony's vision blurred, he did not even feel pain, a wave caught him and was pulling him in every direction. When it was over, he opened his eyes. The Arab was still there. "Hayet is my sister," he told him. Then he kicked him one last time in the hip and walked away. Tony sat up, there on the ground. Blood was running from his nose. He picked up his gun and slipped it into his belt. Then he limped away. From the sidewalk cafés, a good dozen people were watching him.

Neither Dominique nor Vincent was particularly moved by his misadventure. After four years of hostility that had been kept under the surface, a confrontation was inevitable, and there were more pressing questions to settle. Besides, they told him, he had gone looking for trouble. Tony felt terribly wounded and humiliated. He poured out his heart to Stéphane. He had thought he could count on his buddies and it seemed that was not the case, the first Arab who came along could do anything he wanted, and everyone figured that was normal. Dominique and Vincent's attitude disappointed him deeply. Stéphane said he understood. Maybe they could settle the issue without anyone else's help, especially since there were other reasons to act besides the attack he had fallen victim to. According to what Stéphane knew, Hayet's brother was selling drugs, and in the past, the movement had taken radical measures against dealers, and those measures could be brought back. Justice would be served.

"Are you talking about those two Tunisians from Ajaccio?" Tony asked.

"Yes."

"You want us to kill the Arab, is that it?" he asked again.

"Don't you want to see him dead?" Stéphane asked in return.

Tony pictured all those people sitting at their tables who had watched him walk away painfully and said nothing while blood spurted out of his nose. And he thought of the mess his nose was in.

"Yes," he answered. "Yes, I do!"

They checked on a few details and set up a meeting one evening the following week. Tony was a little overwrought, but Stéphane had attained a state of extraordinary lucidity. A man hardens himself by coming up against hard things. That's how he learns to know himself. Yes, he was lucid, without illusions. There was something tender and almost feminine in him that he had to get rid of, something that gave his feelings of friendship a servile, submissive air, something that meant that no-one thought of him for virile actions, something that would die tonight at the same time as that man he had never seen. They waited until the restaurant where Hayet's brother worked had closed. They let a half hour go by, then slipped silently into the flea-bitten stairway of the old building where the employees had their rooms. They stopped in front of a wooden door and heard raï music. They checked their pistols fitted with silencers. They were wearing balaclavas pushed up on their foreheads. Tony started to lower his but Stéphane shook his head. He knocked on the door. It opened a moment later. Tony recognised the man who had attacked him and blocked the door with his foot, then pushed the door back hard. The Arab lost his balance. Tony and Stéphane fired at the same time. The Arab staggered and collapsed in the Turkish toilets, his back to the wall. They moved into the room to finish him off. On their left, sitting on a bed, another Arab was looking at them, his mouth open. Stéphane stepped up to him and shot him twice in the head. He motioned to Tony to do the same with his attacker. Tony was frozen. Stéphane did the shooting for him. He breathed deeply and looked around. On the wall, above the bed, there were bloodstains, shattered bone and brain. The white tiles of the toilet were running with blood. There was blood everywhere. They left and closed the door carefully. Ten minutes later, they were in the car. They had just started driving when Tony rolled down his window fast, stuck his head out and vomited. Once he had dropped him off at his house, Stéphane drove up to the village where Virginie was waiting for him. Tell me, she asked, tell me everything.

The next evening, Vincent and Dominique called the entire group together for a secret meeting in a safe house. They were waiting with a newspaper in their hand. On page one, news of the murder of two Arab drug dealers, complete with their photograph. A dozen bars of hashish ready to be sold had been found in their room. For Dominique and Vincent, there was no doubt: the other side was responsible for the murders, but they could not figure out why. Why, now, would they bring back the war against drugs from the 1980s? To show they were the uncontested and legitimate heirs of the movement? And at a time like this, when they were on the verge of war? That made no sense. Stéphane asked for the floor and announced, as calm as you please, that he, along with Tony, had carried out the executions. Everyone sat in silence. Then they understood that one of the murdered Arabs was Hayet's brother. Why? Dominique asked in a flat voice. Stéphane stood up and launched into a speech, appealing to their uncontested and legitimate heritage, moral cleanliness and the safeguarding of identity, and the more Dominique listened, the more devastated and ashamed he felt, as if these were not words reaching his ears, but viscous splatters of organic matter that he would never be able to wash off, the words heavy, ever heavier and more viscous, they were not Stéphane's words but foul fragments of impersonal and blind speech that had been chewed and digested again and again, and that all Stéphane's years of activism had deposited in his mind until he was transformed into what was now standing before Dominique, this cold-hearted individual who expressed himself so heatedly, this monument of bad faith whose sincerity was total, this new kind of monster whose humanity was so uncontested Dominique could not tolerate the deep shame that washed over him – the shame of being a man like that man. He asked him to stop talking. Then he shone a flashlight on Tony's face, which was still covered with bruises.

"And that," Dominique asked, "does that have anything to do with 'the overwhelming duty to safeguard our identity'?"

"O.K., so Tony had a personal interest, but that's not why we did it," Stéphane said coolly. "And even if it was the case, that would change absolutely nothing about the validity of the political motives I've explained to you as clearly as I could. On the contrary. Everyone has to know that no-one can touch our guys, and that we'll defend them if necessary. That's two good reasons right there. It was an initiative that had to be taken. Especially at a time like this."

Dominique announced that the meeting was adjourned. He could not stand it anymore. He asked Vincent to stay. They were alone in the empty house.

"We have to expel those two bastards right away," Dominique said.

Vincent did not reply straightaway. He lit a cigarette in the darkness.

"I don't think that's a good idea. Not now. If it had been another time, I would have agreed with you absolutely, and I'm sad for the girl, you know that, and you also know that things are going to turn sour and that it's vital, Dumè, vital that we show no signs of our internal divisions."

"Are you joking?"

"No. I'm not. It would be a big mistake, not only because it would weaken us, but it would also be bad for group morale. Don't fool yourself, out of those guys, no-one gives a shit about the two Arabs, and I'm willing to bet people think Stéphane and Tony have got balls, it's as simple as that, and besides, I wouldn't be surprised if they did it so everyone knows they've got balls. That's why I'm telling you it's not a good idea. On any level. We need everyone we have. Trouble is coming, it's going to be terrible and you know it."

"Terrible?" Dominique echoed.

He did not know what to say. Shame darkened his spirit. He went home. Vannina was asleep. He lay down next to her and held her so tight she woke up. She kissed his eyelids and ran her hand through his hair. He breathed in her scent and felt they were alone in their embrace, the only island of life floating in a universe of death. Dumè, she said, Dumè, what's the matter? He did not answer, he held her close, he pressed his face against her breasts and clung with all his might to her small graceful body, her fragile body against his, the only rampart that could protect him against the silent hostility of a world of ghosts. They had never had a child. For years, Dominique made love to her thinking of that child who had never come, he moved inside her, he opened his eyes and gazed into her eyes, and thought about the child. He had stopped thinking about it.

He did not need to. He thought only of her. It was better that way.

"I don't know what to do," he said softly.

"Whatever you do will be done well," she said as she cradled him.

The next day, they went to see Hayet. Vannina paid her respects with great warmth and sincerity. But he could not do the same. He stammered out something about being sorry and saw that she took his discomfort as indifference. He could not do anything about it. He was too ashamed. He went to see Vincent.

"I quit," he told him. "I'm quitting everything. Right now."

"You can't quit now. You can't do that to us. Not because of that business. You're too important. We need you."

"I can't fight anymore, not with you and not for you. To the man you've turned into, I can't even explain why. That man wouldn't understand."

"Oh, I understand, alright! You have principles. Fucking stupid principles, as usual. You and your conscience. Your pristine soul. You don't really give a shit about the circumstances, right? You do what you judge is right, and you're so sure of yourself you don't see that what's right, in certain circumstances, like now, is a mistake. A really ugly mistake."

"I've thought about it. If anyone threatens you, if you're in danger, you, just you, understand that I'll be there. I'll always be there. And you know it."

Vincent was touched despite his anger.

"That's not good enough," he said. "But thanks anyway. Thanks, Dumè."

"Don't thank me, Vincent. I have to be faithful to something. Everything's changed, everything's fucked, but I have to be faithful to something. That's why, out of fidelity. Otherwise, as far as I'm concerned, if you really want to know, you're all worthless and you can all go and croak. You and the rest of them."

Talk to me, please, talk to me, Virginie moaned, tell me again. And let me touch you. Stéphane told her of the luminous colour of blood, its true colour, not the faded traces old blood leaves in dusty archives. New blood brings back the old. There is new language, new movement, a new world. Freedom is total, freedom destroys, it is apocalyptic. Stéphane earned it, he earned the right to be admired, he justified the possession of everything that was given to him ahead of time, and freely, everything was justified now. He had the right to his pleasure. In the hand of the Archangel, God placed a sword. At the deepest point of love shines the steel of a glittering blade. He who fights for Good must first free himself from the demands of Good. He had earned the right without which no struggle will triumph. And he had the right to wallow in the blood he needed to spill like an anthropophagic divinity. He was not confined to respect and worship anymore, sitting on his chair, his worship was freed too, and he could take his pleasure with an angel, as long as he found pleasure in a new way. The pleasure must be new, and it can be barbarous. There is no turning back. We will never make love. Why? Why? Virginie cried, she moaned. Because it is beneath us, too far beneath us. Because I love you. Do you love me? Virginie asked, and she sighed interminably. Yes, I love you, I don't even know how to tell you. Next time, I will bring you something better than words, something I will bring for you only and that you alone will see. Trust me. The next time? Yes – next time.

"Do you know what happened at Pila-Canale in the 1860s?" Stéphane asked.

"No," Tony said. "And I don't care."

"I'll tell you anyway. A vendetta started between two families in the village, it started out as enmity, you see, they avoided meeting, they stopped talking. When the vendetta per se started, one of the families didn't answer back right away. They lay low in their house and did nothing. Their enemies were in a rage, you see, because the other side didn't respond to their violence. They accused them of being cowards, they killed the men who rented their land, they slaughtered their animals, you see?"

"I see," Tony said. "And they let it happen?"

"In the family that didn't defend itself, one of the sons, the oldest, I think, the father's favourite, thought they could make peace, could convince their enemies to come to a friendly agreement, you see, the guy wasn't too hot on fighting. But his opinion didn't carry the day and they finally decided they would have to have this vendetta. And you know what the first thing they did was, do you have any idea?"

"No," Tony said.

"The men of the family walked onto the village square, all of them together. The oldest son was there too, the favourite. His brothers grabbed him, his brothers, Tony, and they forced him to kneel, right there in the square, and his father slit his throat. Behind the closed shutters, everyone watched. And they left him there, on the village square."

Tony said nothing.

"I know history's not your thing, Tony, but I'm sure you can guess. In your opinion, which side won the vendetta?"

Tony had no answer.

"We're going to kill Dominique Guerrini, Tony, we're going to kill that asshole of a traitor. You and me."

Dominique Guerrini's coffin faced the altar and his wife stared at it. The entire village was in the church. Vincent Leandri was the only nationalist militant there. The others had not forgiven Dominique's desertion. Marie-Angèle and Virginie Susini were in the second row. In her purse, Virginie was carrying the photograph Stéphane had given her three days earlier. He had told her how, when Dominique fell, he did not cry out, not a sound, he brought his knees up towards his chest, he waved his hand in the air, as if pushing something away, and tried to wrap his arms around his legs. Stéphane took the photograph for Virginie. And then Dominique died. Or maybe he was already dead. Everything happened quickly and easily. They waited for Dominique to leave the bar and walk a few metres away, and when they were sure no-one could see him from inside, they fired on him with silencers on their guns. Though there was no need, since the beginning of the confrontation, the bar had been deserted. Dominique was the only one who had kept going there regularly, maybe because he thought he had nothing more to lose, or out of pride, or because he could not change his habits, after all, he was on his territory, there was no other place in the world where he felt safer. That was why they chose to kill him there. Marie-Angèle and Hayet had found his body a good half hour later, when they closed the bar. Marie-Angèle screamed and the whole village came running. Vannina Guerrini burst out of her house and the people kept her from seeing the body. Now she was standing before the coffin, crying softly, on and off. She was not anyone's rampart anymore. She stood straight, her hands on the back of the prie-dieu. Virginie thought she was magnificently beautiful. She could not take her eyes off her. At the end of the Mass, right before the condolences, when the coffin was taken out, Vannina began howling like an animal, she would not accept this thing, people pressed around her to support and comfort her. Vincent stood in the corner and looked elsewhere. He lined up with the others to present his condolences. Virginie was ahead of him. He saw her embrace Dominique's wife with all her heart, and kiss her several times with a warmth and compassion that was a wonder to see. When his turn came, he gave her an impersonal, fleeting kiss. He could do no more. The only thing that counted would be the years to come, those two years during which the dark heart would go on beating without anyone hearing, the years of Virginie's mortal anguish, the years of fear and monotony, the years of incommensurable disillusionment, the years of Virginie's ecstasy and Stéphane's victorious ascension, until that day in 1996 when the constant threats stopped supplying a reason for living, when a new memory had to be invented, and when Tony, who had no more fear of death, began to keep a vigil in the silent darkness of his room, convinced that the ghosts that had been liberated, knowing he was available, would finally come and demand a settling of accounts, and he would be able to explain to them what had occurred, even if he did not really know what he would tell them, he kept his vigil for nights on end, he fought sleep with all his strength and smiled at the strange shadows insomnia drew in the darkness, but no-one came, there were no ghosts, and he was alone with his explanations that no-one wanted, with his livid insomnia and his nights in which even nightmares deserted him. Then he put an end to the absence of remorse and the silence by hanging himself from a beam in his basement on that night in 1996, very close to the one Virginie would never forget, the one that, every day, she had prayed for piously, when she went to meet Stéphane in an apartment in town, amazed he had survived to love her still, she understood how much he loved her, and how much further their love went compared to all the past and future loves on this earth, beyond human understanding, that night she knocked on the door of a strange apartment, and a strange girl opened the door and took her by the hand and walked her into the living room, to Stéphane who was smiling, lying on a sofa in a room flooded with lamplight, and she sat down and watched Stéphane's hands reach for the girl and undress her, and she closed her eyes, not daring to watch, closed her eyes as tightly as she could, until the voice rose up, the only voice she adored that told her, full of sweetness and compassion, my heart, no, not tonight, my heart, yes, tonight, open your eyes, sit there, don't move – but open your eyes.

Look. Now you can look at me.

"BEHIND YOU, THE SEA ..."

Do I have a better life? It's hard to tell. I often dream of Balco Atlantico. In my dream, no-one is playing flamenco, no lovers are quarrelling and no children are laughing, Khaled isn't even there. I am alone facing the ocean. There is the sound of the waves and, growing louder, the drumming of a galloping horse. I am missing something but I don't know what. Khaled is beginning to feel the weight of disillusionment. He is nervous. Maybe Mama was right about him: he is unable to know happiness. Maybe he was born with the evil eye.

His job at the restaurant irritates him. The invisible walls he keeps running into irritate him. Only Ryad and I find favour in his eyes.

Remember, Hayet, back home, on the place de la Libération? There was a wall that cut across it too. Everyone acted like there was a wall. We never went to the side where the fancy cafés were, never. We stayed next to the gate to the medina, in a cloud of kif smoke. With the whores and the fishing nets. Even if we all lived in the same town. But it wasn't the same town. There were several towns and no path between them. There is no god but God, but he filled his creation with borders that chop it up in pieces. Here and everywhere else.

Maybe we shouldn't have come then. If it's the same here.

Don't be silly. We're still better off here.

But I think he doesn't believe that anymore. My heart hurts for him because I understand him. And I know there is nothing I can do. We won't change the world. We won't erase its borders to make everything one. Vincent Leandri is still very nice to me. He knows I have a brother since he often takes me down to the town so I can see him, but he doesn't think twice about it. He is devoted and seems to have affection for me, but he never shows any desire to have a coffee with my brother, and he doesn't ask any questions about him. Marie-Angèle either. It's like Khaled didn't exist. Like with our father. And now we can't dream of a place where things would be different.

He is trying to figure out a way to bring hashish from Morocco. He would like to ask a Moroccan who has papers and is going back for vacation with his family. But no-one has papers. He thinks he might call someone in Larache who could slip some into our uncle's car, the next time he goes to visit, without our uncle being the wiser. He knows that would be unforgivable, but still, he gave up the idea reluctantly. He is full of anger and frustration.

One night, at the bar in the village, Tony Versini was very drunk. He looks at me strangely a lot of the time, but he's never acted wrong with me. I was cleaning a table near him. When I leaned over with my rag, I felt a hand on my backside. I turned around fast. It was Tony. He winked at me. Nobody saw anything. The humiliation was horrible. I asked him what was wrong with him. He started to laugh and put his arm around my waist to pull me closer. I tried to get free but he held me tighter and I felt his hand trying to slip into my pants. I screamed as loud as I could, pushed him away, and slapped him. In the bar, everything went quiet. He grabbed me by the arm, I felt his fingers digging into my biceps. He hurt me. No-one reacted. I've never felt so alone. I wanted to cry. I wanted to walk along the ocean with my brother. Far from here.

"What the hell are you doing, you dirty whore, you shitty little Arab?"

Marie-Angèle told him to let me go. He didn't. Vincent Leandri pushed him away hard. Don't you touch her. You should be ashamed. Tony stood there in silence. Sorry, he said. I don't know what came over me. Sorry.

Marie-Angèle was very angry. She said it was the first time anyone had done something like that in her bar and she never expected that he, Tony, knowing him as she did, would be the one to do it. He understood, Vincent said, he understood. At the counter, Dominique Guerrini and Stéphane Campana said nothing. I had to go back to work. I was so tired. Marie-Angèle told me I could go to my room and lie down.

The next day, Khaled realised I wasn't doing well. He asked me what was wrong. I tried not to answer, but I started to cry. I asked him what we were doing here and where our better lives had gone. I couldn't stop crying. He didn't know what to say, I was so sorry for him. He saw the bruise that Tony's fingers made on my arm.

Who did that to you, Hayet, who did that?

Nobody. What could you do about it?

Is that why you're crying? Who did that to you? I want you to tell me who.

No.

He looked at my arm and I felt all his fury and frustration boiling up. I felt all his love too and I cried even harder.

It's nothing.

He held me in his arms. Alright, it's nothing.

It's nothing. It's the kind of thing that ends up happening in bars, it's a miracle it didn't happen before, but I swear, everything was settled as well as it could have been. But I'm just so tired, and little things affect me. I don't know what I'm doing here. I don't understand what all this means.

Are you mad at me for bringing you here?

No, Khaled, I'm not mad at you. I can't even say I regret that I left. If I could really regret I wouldn't be so lost.

I understand. Let's not talk about it anymore.

He told me he'd given up trying to bring hashish from

Morocco but that he'd met a guy who would give him some to sell for a percentage, not much. Ryad would help and they'd share what they earned.

I went back to work. Tony didn't show up at the bar for a week.

Ryad and Khaled got the hashish. They are going to make a little money.

Come and have lunch with us tomorrow. We'll go to the Moroccan restaurant that just opened. The food will be crap, but we'll have fun.

I agreed. We ate with Ryad. We laughed because the cooking was so bad. But the wine was good. Khaled was happy again. He had recovered some hope and dignity. He was like a little boy. He put everyone in a good mood.

When I went to meet Vincent Leandri, who was going to drive me back to the village, Khaled held me very tight. Ryad kissed me on the cheek too. I walked away and I felt their presence behind me. I turned around and they were waving their arms in the air. Khaled's smile was so beautiful. With my fingertips, I blew them one more kiss.

MEMORY OVERLOAD

(1991–85)

When you get to a new place, at first, there is plenty to do. You are fascinated by life. The students drinking in the bars, the night starry with lights, music everywhere. You hear singing, the mournful tune of a guitar, an Irish jig, rhythm and melancholy, set loose from the fiddles. You feel like it's all moving towards a common goal, the good-hearted will to live together, and knowing how, knowing why. That made me happy. At least for a time. As I waited to find a house, I fucked at the hotel. Mornings I arrived at my office, whistling a tune. The students wanted to work with me. Stéphane Campana asked to meet me. Evenings I visited the bars, I did not sleep alone and when I did, it was alright because I fell asleep in the sparkling lights and the echo of distant music. But all that was fake, of course. Something pernicious and sombre was beating like a heart in the guitars and the fiddles, splitting the common goal and the good-hearted will until they exploded with a bang. At night, in the hallways of the university residence, you heard cries of despair and laughter. In the morning you discovered windowpanes broken by fists, blood everywhere, little chunks of flesh hanging on jagged glass. The students' hands were covered with weeping blisters where they had put out their cigarettes. They hated each other as a group. Yes, it was hatred. Of themselves, of others, of everything. When I gave a class, terrible hostility hung over the room. Worst was the sadness. The students loved me because I let them say whatever they wanted and made them feel like they were geniuses, but their love was empty, it was abstract and without foundation, whereas the hostility and sadness spread in a terribly real and concrete way. They did not hate me because I played no role in their ruined world.

I began to think of her. I awaited her forgiveness. I wanted her to forgive me for having abandoned her or, perhaps, already, without knowing it, I wanted her to forgive me for not letting her live. I remembered how, when I was young, I already thought about her, as if she were watching out, at the infinite threshold of possible worlds, for the moment when I would open the door to her becoming real. I was with a young woman, I had promised her a child, no, not a child, I had promised her Sarah, I was lying on top of this young woman, I was moving inside her, she was looking at me with trust and love and I, in the duplicity of my soul, I prayed with all my might for Sarah not to come, for her to forever stay far from me, even as I moved, and smiled, and said nothing, and I knew I would go to hell for that, I knew it would be a liquid hell like in my childhood nightmares, the world would sink and disappear like water into sand, I would be afraid, but no maternal hand would succour me and I would be alone forever, far from my child who would not exist. I remembered the young woman, I remembered my thoughts and fears, but I could not place that moment in my life. That did not worry me. Among all the women I had known in my accommodating cowardice, there must have been one I'd promised to have a child with, though with no real intention of keeping my promise, just to have some peace and quiet. But which woman? When? I had no idea.

I remember a certain October morning. I am not sure this memory is trustworthy, but I've said that does not matter anymore and I have to stand by that. Day was dawning. The sky was clear and it was very cold. Snow and sheets of ice covered the ground. I was alone on the place Paoli. Strangely, the cafés were not opening and there was no sound of the town awakening. Only silence. I saw the dark opening of the Restonica river valley with its jagged rocks, the shadow of the citadel perched on its height, and all around me, the blue silhouette of the mountains, this massive presence enveloped me in silence, the cold, the pure blue sky, and I felt everything was about to crack, collapse and bury me. I was not afraid. Something solemn and sacred was at work. I walked through the sleeping town. Sitting on a drystone wall, in a narrow lane I have never been able to find again, a little girl was staring at me with serious eyes. She was Sarah's age. We were the only ones keeping watch over the sleeping town.

I did not speak to her. I do not remember what I did the rest of the day. It is as if it ended there, suddenly, very early in the morning.

That day has been lost to me. But I have not stopped thinking of my little girl. I have let other people's faces fade, as if an eraser were slowly rubbing out the features of the woman who might have loved me and the boys whose father I did not wish to be. But I thought of Sarah, I thought of her all the time, and I forgot the violence that fed off the heavy silence around me, I thought of Sarah and said to her, there was a day, I'm sure, when I let you come to me, remember, I stopped praying you would remain a prisoner of nothingness, I called you and you came, the way a child comes to a father when he calls. But since then, call as I might, she does not come. I knew I should not have fled. I knew I should not have been what I am. But that knowledge was useless. I was not worthy of it.

In the end, I have no reason to complain. I, who never really felt guilty, received no punishment. My distress and solitude were not punishments. How could I have known at the time that Marie-Angèle was waiting for me and that, one day, I would not need to run anymore because I would be freed from desire and fear? If I had known, I would have agreed to pay the price, and ahead of time. A measly amount. I live surrounded by archives. My memory has become a labyrinth, an immense depository filled with the memories of the man I could have been, all the memories that other men unknown to me have abandoned or refuse to recognise, a place of traitors and reprobates, a girl waiting to be born reigns over it with a ghost on a cold and splendid autumn morning, the victims calling for retribution jostle other victims who are silent, smiling idiots and legionnaires paralysed by love, I console my little girl who is crying, I am a father above reproach and I console her for a nightmare she never had. I can live with all that, no problem. There is plenty of room.

But I did not know that yet. Time had expanded without my knowing. I had just moved into a fine house on the road to Aléria that I had chosen for its isolation, to escape the sinister festivities and false agitation of the town. I had been living there for a few days. I had brought university girls there and a woman from the faculty. They had slept with me. That evening, for the first time, I was alone. I poured myself two or three strong drinks to calm my anxiety, but that did not work. Darkness was falling and I heard my heart beating as night drew near. I tried in vain to remember who that woman was, when I was younger and would not give her Sarah, and I started to be afraid because I would have to sleep alone. Then, by the door, the air began to tremble and darken, it slowly condensed with a rustling of faded lace, and I saw, ever more clearly, a pale overcoat and, beneath a leather three-cornered hat, the cruel glow of a transparent smile. A tender, depraved voice spoke. I was transported by beatitude and terror. I should have understood I was saved.

"BEHIND YOU, THE SEA ..."

I often hear your voice. I am so afraid I may be mistaken. Didn't you laugh once and say, you know, Hayet, Tariq ibn Ziyad never conquered Andalusia. He stayed in Larache, our town, with his wife and children. Every evening, they went for a walk on Balco Atlantico, which had already been built back then, in the early days of Islam. He never was a conqueror. When he came home late, he was afraid his wife would scold him. But no-one told us that. We learn his speech by heart, we know the meaning of the name "Gibraltar," we think of him, but these are lies. I have revealed the truth to you. They lied to us out of love. They made memories for us so we would feel less ashamed of ourselves, the way I have lied to you so often, trusting in your love and forgiveness.

Didn't you tell me that – I'm so afraid my memories of you are lies? There are so many lies. The day after your death, the newspapers published your photograph. I had taken it one spring day on Balco Atlantico. They must have found it in your things. They had no right. They wrote that two Arab dealers had been murdered in their room. That was all. In the articles, they made it sound like it was a form of natural justice. That is what will remain of your life, and Ryad's – and my life too. Our lives will be related by people who know nothing of the wonderful stories you would tell me as we watched the sun dive into the Atlantic. People who never discovered a harvest of severed heads on the threshold of their house, who never woke up sweating in the threatening solitude of a murderous night. They know nothing and they get to write our epitaphs.

I waited for condolences and compassion. Blessed are you to have died and not seen what I received! Only Marie-Angèle took me in her arms with some spontaneity. The others looked embarrassed. Vincent Leandri never met my eyes again and never told me anything except what he wanted to drink. Dominique Guerrini and his wife came and said they were sorry for me. And when, two months after you, Dominique was killed in front of the bar, I couldn't help think he got what he deserved because you were dead too. I became evil. May God keep me that way.

I should have stopped my story a long time ago. I wasn't near you for your last moments. But I can't help imagining them.

After leaving me forever, though you did not know it, you went to have tea with Ryad. Then you both went to work. In the kitchen, you were in a good mood and you laughed a lot. The night was slow and you could get to bed early. You each lay down on your bed. Maybe you had a cigarette. Ryad thought of his promise, and his mother's relief, and he was able to smile. If you let me believe it, I will say you were dreaming of walking with me on Balco Atlantico, and we were watching the most sumptuous sunset God ever brought to this earth since the first day of creation. It was so wondrous that you stopped seeing walls everywhere. For the first time you saw the silent fishing boats far below, returning to the harbour, the blazing horizon, the soft beacon of the lighthouse coming to life. You were dreaming. The world was full of beauty and I was your loving sister.

And now God has withdrawn His hand from above our heads. They knocked on the door to your room. God withdrew His hand, and I want to believe that, in His infinite mercy, he spared you from fear. They knocked very softly. On his bed, Ryad did not even open his eyes. I believe it was you, Khaled, enchanted by the infinite softness of the knocking, who rose and opened the door to death. Until the last second, God allowed it not to be death. First it was an eager young fiancée whose tender hand brushed the closed door to her first rendezvous with love. Then, once the door was open, it was a horse galloping on the waves that carried you off in a gust of wind.

A YOUNG GIRL'S DREAM

(October 2000)

Lying on his bed, Vincent turned towards the photograph he had set on his night table the evening before. He reached out his hand and picked it up. He forced himself to look at it again until he was sure he was finally crying and that he had understood something. The soul had been lost long ago, even before the tragedy, but he had not realised it, so he did not suffer unduly. He had done what was necessary. Not go home at a set time. Not travel on the same roads. Be careful when stepping out of the car. Squeeze the grip of a loaded pistol, though that was useless. Wars end and people survive. How long had Vincent been happy to have survived? He did not recall. He did not remember having been happy or relieved. His soul was lost, there was neither happiness nor relief. Everything seemed strange. As strange as Dominique's coffin and his bereaved wife's muffled sobs. When the body was being taken to the cemetery, she let out an endless cry, she howled no, oh, no, but dozens of hands reached for her and held her fast so she could receive the condolences, still standing, at the door to the church, according to convention, while her husband was taken from her. The tears were distant, the cry was distant, they signified nothing, and Vincent was surprised not to find within himself the grief he sought. He thought maybe it was because Dominique and he were no longer friends the last time they saw each other. He thought he was still angry with him. But that wasn't it. His soul was lost, the mourning of loving wives was a mystery, like love and grief. The common language had disappeared. He considered trying to rebuild the movement. Weeks passed and he realised he had no desire to do so. Everything seemed wearisome, useless, devoid of interest. He felt no pain. Someone was erasing the contours of the world. It wasn't hell, it wasn't damnation, there was no suffering or, if it was hell, not knowing you were damned was part of the punishment, simply his soul was lost and things lay motionless, bled out, in a universe without contours. Vincent watched Stéphane act enthusiastically and speak with conviction. It was monotonous and painful. He did not understand. More often than not, he couldn't find the energy to attend meetings. No-one missed him. Finally he stopped going altogether. He spent his days at the bar. He could not take his eyes off Hayet, but he could not meet her gaze. The militants, even those who had admired him so deeply, greeted him with palpable contempt. Stéphane had stopped bothering to speak with him. His feelings were not hurt. His pride, unwounded. He stood with one elbow on the counter, and when Hayet washed glasses or made coffee, he watched her. When she turned his way, he lowered his head. She must have noticed, but she said nothing. Maybe, without realising it, he was trying to be ashamed in front of her, but in vain. For his soul was lost and his heart continued to beat like mad. Every day, he pictured the Indian Ocean and the eyes of the zebu. He liked talking about that with Théodore Moracchini, he didn't know why. Now, with the photograph in his hand, he understood. The memory of life, the shame, the suffering and love recovered the meaning they once had. His lost soul sent him a painful message and Vincent, crying again the way humans cry, full of gratitude and sadness, thought he was finally going to regain that soul.

At that very moment, Stéphane Campana, fighting a migraine, left for Ajaccio. The October day promised to be abnormally warm, like high summer. When he awoke, nauseated, Stéphane knew what to expect, and he was in a wretched mood. He berated his wife for not having made coffee, he told her he was going to be late because of her, and that she had put on weight. He considered that seeing her cry might bring him relief, but she lowered her eyes and said nothing. The hot coffee nearly made him vomit. He choked down a spasm that made the blood pound in his temples, and pain shot through him like lightning. It was hopeless, but he took two aspirin. With every move, his liquefied brain slapped against the walls of his skull like molten lava in a crater. He moaned as his car engine turned over. He had married two years ago, though he did not love the woman he had chosen.

That was not his problem. He wanted a normal love life, he wanted to be free of Virginie. When he told her he was going to marry another woman, she did not make a fuss. She looked at him in silence with her usual serious face, and he felt such malaise he could not help but lie to her. Cursing his cowardice, he promised he would go on seeing her, he told her their love was greater than any social convention and deserved to be safeguarded from the filth of conjugal arrangements, he told her nothing would change. Stéphane didn't know he wasn't lying. Because nothing did change and he went on seeing Virginie. Three days after the ceremony, he called her. And he saw her regularly. He could not help himself. Every time, he promised himself it would have to stop, it was the last time he would call her, he left her place feeling as dirty as if he had wallowed in a trash heap, but there was nothing he could do, hours went by, disgust disappeared and everything that had disgusted him filled him now with irrepressible, unhealthy excitement, he wanted to see her lying on the bed with her eyes blindfolded, split like the carcass of an animal, he wanted to see her open her legs and do everything he asked without protesting, but without enthusiasm, without abandoning that attitude of perverse gravitas that horrified him and filled him with desire so intolerable he grabbed the telephone and called her again. As he drove, he thought of her, he could not help it. Suddenly the car skidded. He held onto the wheel with all his strength and hit the brakes. The car stopped.

Stéphane felt his heart pounding, and his migraine reached its peak. He stepped out and saw that a tyre had blown in the rutted road. He went and fetched the jack. The sun burned the back of his neck. Fat drops of dirty sweat fell onto the overheated asphalt. It was torture. When he had tightened the last nut, Stéphane moaned with relief. He was about to open the door when his foot slipped on something. A foul smell rose up. He spent the next fifteen minutes using a little stick to try and clear from the treads of his shoe the dog shit he had stepped in. He tried not to vomit. Incessant drumming clattered in his skull. He imagined cool dawns and clear skies, the scent of damp earth. Pain pretended to recede, then returned to torture him again. With it came terribly graphic visons of Virginie. The sun was pitiless.

That must have been two years earlier, maybe less, not long after Stéphane Campana got married, but Vincent did not remember exactly when. That night he had drunk a lot, even more than usual. Hayet had her back turned and he could look at her all he wanted. He imagined talking to her, making her smile, it was all a little vague, she would press her body against his, but then he caught himself and escaped the trap of his imagination. What would he have said to her? That she had lived and was still living among her brother's murderers? That in 1996, without warning, Tony Versini hanged himself? He had left a note, completely incomprehensible: "Never ghosts". When you knew him as well as Vincent thought he did, it was hard to understand how Tony could have gone that far. Nothing seemed more out of character than life-and-death dramas, or even ordinary mental anguish. There must have been a purely physical explanation, a wiring defect, a cerebral connection that had gone haywire and produced that aberrant result. That would not have consoled Hayet. Especially if she learned that the other murderer was very much alive, she rubbed shoulders with him all the time, and he, Vincent, knew all about it. How could he have made her smile? How could he have believed she would not run from his touch? Gazing at her in silence – that was his only option. It was midnight. Théodore Moracchini had gone back to his house earlier in the evening. Sitting alone at a table, Virginie was paging through a fashion magazine. Fatigue finally caught up with Vincent. "Good night," he said, heading for the door. "Good night," Hayet said, and did not turn around. He was on his way home when he heard someone walking behind him. Virginie.

"Can I come back with you for a minute, Vincent? I have something to tell you."

He had agreed. He was not even curious. It was easier to agree than find an acceptable reason to say no. At his place, he asked if she wanted something to drink. No. Then he asked what she wanted to tell him. She motioned to him to come closer. When he was very close, she looked at him for a moment, very serious and self-possessed, and kissed him on the mouth. He pulled away. She took his arm, looked at him again very carefully, and kissed him once more on the mouth. Her kiss was cold. Her eyes were open and her lips nearly closed. Vincent had not touched a woman for a very long time. His soul was lost, but his heart had gone on beating in an empty body. There was no reason to refuse. She let him take her into the bedroom. She removed her clothes. Her pubic hair was just starting to grow back. She came to him on the bed. She would not let him turn off the light. There was no warmth, no sighs. She would not let him kiss her again. He had trouble penetrating her. None of it moved him, he had forgotten the moments of modesty and abandonment, the way life can leap forward. He had forgotten it all, he had floated so long in the limbo of monotony, he had forgotten how to recognise the face of sadness. As he manipulated her in mechanical fashion, Virginie never stopped watching, and he never saw her blink. When it was over, she propped herself up on one elbow and examined Vincent's naked body. He tried to hold her, since his body had retained the rituals of tenderness in its memory, but she pushed him away.

"What are you doing? You're trying to get revenge on Stéphane, is that it? Because he got married? You chose me because you think I'm the guy he couldn't stand you sleeping with?"

She sat up suddenly.

"Stéphane will never find out," she swore. "Never! If you tell him, I don't know what I'll do to you!"

He shrugged and went for his cigarettes in the kitchen. When he came back, Virginie was lying on her back, her legs slightly spread, with no embarrassment, as if she were elsewhere. He saw the streaks of blood. He thought she might be having her period and that he had not realised it. Then he understood. He was amazed.

"You were a virgin?" he asked.

She did not answer. She did not change the way she lay. Absent-mindedly, with her fingertips, she drew patterns with the blood that stained her thigh.

"You were a virgin?" he asked again.

No answer. Vincent started to laugh.

"What exactly has Campana been doing to you since you were thirteen?"

Virginie stood up. She got dressed slowly. When she saw the blood on her hands, she frowned and disappeared into the bathroom. She came back a minute later and stood in front of Vincent who was smoking naked in the middle of the room.

"Tell me, how long has it been since you last fucked?"

"A while," Vincent admitted, shrugging.

"You like fucking? Do you want to fuck again?"

The vulgar word was artificial in her mouth, the way she

repeated it with malicious insistence. Vincent was embarrassed for her. He told her he wouldn't mind.

"Then don't say another thing about Stéphane, ever. You don't even have the right to say the name of a man like him. You don't understand anything. Not a thing. If you say a single word, if you even say his name, I'll never come back and you'll die like a dog. Understand? Get it?"

Rage twisted her face. Vincent closed his eyes and breathed in a lungful of smoke. He thought, without bitterness, that a few years ago, he would have slapped her – or spanked her bare bottom. But that wasn't really it. A few years ago, no-one would have spoken to him this way. He told her he understood.

She returned twice a week. She made love to him with studied hatred. She stared at him with empty eyes, always open, unmoving like the fathomless gaze of the zebu. Depth is fathomless, stupidity is fathomless, the immensity of animal night. On the shores of the Indian Ocean, the girls did not love him either. The girls in the movement did not love him, nor did the waitresses. Something pushed girls into his arms, but it was never love. Still, there must have been affection somewhere, or admiration, or the innocence of desire, the respite of human warmth, or the sheer sincerity of misunderstanding, something besides her methodical, icy insistence, her two eyes opening onto the void. The soul is lost, you do what is necessary. At times, Virginie's expression changed ever so slightly. She would be lying on the bed, in her face he could read disturbance, her eyes would cloud over as if something were fluttering in the darkness of her pupils, and her tight lips seemed to hold back a sigh. Vincent was struck by the truth: how unhappy she must be. He stayed on his side of the bed. No road led to her.

On the evening before that burning October day, Vincent thought it might not be completely inappropriate to try and show he was human for once. He was smoking as usual next to Virginie, who kept her silence. There was no heaviness. She was simply there, with her serious look and her open eyes, and suddenly, very briefly, she collapsed into herself, she hid her face in her hands and breathed a sigh, unutterably sad, almost a sob. Then she recovered and went back to staring into the void as if nothing had happened. Vincent placed his hand on her leg, and she considered that hand with some surprise before pushing it away. He tried to smile.

"You should do something for yourself," he told her in a soft voice.

She looked at him questioningly.

"I mean, for your life."

She was listening now.

"Don't you want something else? Something besides coming here and sleeping with a guy you don't love, that you don't even respect, that you have nothing to say to? How old are you? Twenty-one, twenty-two? Haven't you thought there could be something else?"

She went on looking at him. He expected her to tell him to shut up and mind his own business. He figured he had done what he had to do and that was enough. Then he saw Virginie's eyelashes tremble. Two big shiny tears swelled under her eyelids, then rolled down her cheeks. The body retains the memory of the rituals of tenderness, and Vincent took her in his arms the way he would have embraced a little sister. She started crying harder and did not push him away.

No let-up. The sun struck the windshield. Stéphane tried to calm his breathing. That did not work. He thought for a few seconds that it would, and now he just felt worse. He wanted to turn back, go home, and lie down in the dark, but that was impossible. Too many things to do in Ajaccio. The inside of the car stank. He opened the windows, but that wasn't enough. He felt like tearing his head off his shoulders to put an end to the pain and the stench, he could not tell one from the other. When he arrived, he went to the bank. The movement's money. The legal money. The illegal money. Put things in order. When he walked into his financial advisor's office, he wrinkled up his nose and acted surprised, as if he did not understand where this smell came from that happened to enter the room along with him. Finally he left, relieved and ashamed. He rubbed his sole on the ground. Nothing helped. He thought of buying new shoes but did not have the courage to go into a shop. He stopped by the movement's newspaper. What could be said. What could not be said. What could not be said but must be understood. No-one paid enough attention to detail. He would have to reread everything, which was tiring. No let-up. At noon, in a restaurant, he drank a glass of chilled rosé and the migraine lifted like magic. But when he got up from the table, it came back with twice the violence. He went by the newspaper again to check the articles. People acted as if they knew something and commented on the small semantic changes he had made. He felt their approval, and almost forgot his pain. He had become indispensable. Young people admired him. He was what he had wanted to be. Almost was. He did not want lies. And he kept getting bogged down in lies. You're seeing her! I know you're still seeing her! his wife accused him, and she burst into tears. No, no, I swear, I'm not seeing her, Stéphane answered, with overwhelming sincerity. You still love me, don't you? Virginie asked. Oh, I know you love me! I know you've always loved me, and he told her yes, holding her with all his strength. Lies cannot be avoided. Most of the time people cannot even recognise a lie. Now he was on the telephone. He heard Virginie say hello, he regretted dialling her number, but he said, I'm coming this evening, I'm spending the night with you. Tonight, Virginie said in a small grateful voice, yes, tonight, I am waiting for you. He called his wife, he spoke to her sweetly this time, he told her he had to spend the night in Ajaccio, unfortunately, for an unscheduled political meeting, he was sorry, he missed her, he would be back tomorrow for lunch. He said to her, I love you, you know. That was the last thing she heard him say.

Virginie was starting to be a burden in Vincent's arms. She would not stop crying. The situation was incongruous and he did not want it to last forever. He tried comforting her, but his words were impersonal, senseless formulations that made him even more ill at ease. He repeated the usual things: you'll be alright, you'll see, it won't kill you, you'll find someone who really loves you.

Virginie stopped crying. She pulled away from his arms and stared at him in disbelief.

"Someone who *really* loves me? Because I don't have someone who really loves me now?"

Vincent put up his hands in surrender.

"I'm not allowed to talk about it, sorry, I forgot!" he said, attempting a smile.

"Oh, you are! Today you're allowed. But I want you to answer my question."

"Listen, Virginie, to be honest, I don't give a damn …"

"I want you to answer my question."

Vincent lit a cigarette and shrugged. She was really starting to get on his nerves. Dryly, he told her that, though he was no specialist when it came to people loving each other, really or otherwise, it did seem to him that a guy who hadn't found a way to go to bed with her in nearly ten years and who, on top of that, decided to marry another woman must have, to say the least, a rather minimalist concept of love. But, as he had pointed out, it wasn't his problem, she had his blessing to go on thinking and doing as she pleased.

"He doesn't love me? You're telling me he doesn't love me?"

She looked at him with an expression of pain and hatred that almost made his heart hurt for her. Suddenly she began talking, pouring out endless rivers of words, unbelievably childish, swept along by a current of demented exaltation, as if Vincent had triggered in her a dreadful storm that shook her to her foundations, she grabbed him by the shoulders and drove her nails into his skin to make sure he heard everything she had to say, punctuated by her screaming, he doesn't love me? How can you say he doesn't love me? Vincent listened and his repulsion grew, the portrait she drew of Stéphane and his love for her was so outlandish, she had fallen victim to a cruel bout of destructive fever, the assault of malaria, she paraded cohorts of maddened images that blossomed and grew, fed by the long solitude of a world of darkness, covered with a blindfold, unilluminated by the light of reality, and all those secret images now sprang from the deep darkness of their night, moving like ghosts within Virginie's incessant voice, Stéphane transformed into an epic hero, a knight, a holy healer from the early days of Christianity who stood facing the sea and the unfurling hordes of Islam's warriors, galloping across the waves, a murderous, purifying saint surrounded by cowards and sinners, his power to dole out death had raised him to a height so inconceivable that he stood level with the impassive Divinity, and there was Virginie herself, no longer a pitiful, betrayed young woman, now she was so many other things, the wife of a knight, the priestess of a world at war, an immaterial blind icon at whose feet incense smoked, of whom sacred ritual demanded she be sullied with juices, sperm and blood, a wood nymph for whom her worshippers invented new caresses and changed the meaning of every word, a pagan virgin offered in sacrifice by her family, naked and spread-eagled, to the spirits of underground worlds, above all she was a wife, a mother, a loving sister who accepted the secrets of the man she loved and made them hers so they became of one spirit and one memory. Vincent was appalled when he understood she knew everything about what Stéphane had done, including the murder of the two Arabs. The enormity of the trust he put in her went far beyond what anyone could imagine when it came to carelessness and indiscretion. And she admired him for that.

"He doesn't love me?" Virginie repeated one last time.

"Yes," Vincent admitted to stop her talking. "Yes, he loves you. I take back what I said."

"I'll show you how much he loves me," she said. "Wait right here."

She gathered her clothes. Feverishly, she started getting dressed. She seemed about to collapse at any minute.

"Don't bother," Vincent said. "I believe you. Go home and sleep."

"Wait right here!" She went out of the room.

Vincent was tired. He wondered how he could get rid of her. He had no intention of spending the night making a list of the irrefutable proof of a love that did not involve him. Ten minutes later, Virginie was back.

"He took this photo for me. And he doesn't love me?" she said, handing him a Polaroid.

Curled up, Dominique Guerrini lay in the dust in a position of infinite weakness. His blood formed a dark stain around his body.

"When was this photo taken?" Vincent asked.

He did not need an answer. Virginie gave him a self-satisfied smile. It was intolerable. Vincent heard himself tell her that Stéphane must never set foot in the village again.

"He'll come back," she said, her words a challenge. "No-one can keep him away from me. No-one, especially not you!"

She went home. He lay down and set the photograph on the night table. Strangely, he fell asleep immediately. In the darkness of a silent nightmare, two empty eyes stared at him. Nothing else happened.

*

It wasn't just Dominique but it started with Dominique, dying alone while his murderer took his picture. He looked like a scared little boy. Maybe he did not know who was responsible for his death. Vincent thought it would be better that way. And maybe it was better not to mourn him. If there is a paradise, Vincent thought, it is made for men like Dominique. Then he cried all the harder. The last words they had spoken to each other were harsh, but that did not matter now. There was an immutable essence of friendship safeguarded somewhere at the summit of an invisible sky that harsh words could not damage and death could not alter. In the name of this essence, it was Vincent's duty to come and comfort Dominique who had become a little boy, who had been harmed and could not defend himself alone, take him in and console him in his immense solitude. The weakness of this new child was limitless. And after Dominique there was Hayet, another weakness and another solitude that asked to be taken in, and then, after her, Hayet's brother, whose name Vincent had not thought to ask, and his friend, so pitiful they lived only in a single dull memory, dead in order to feed the morbid fantasies of a poor deceived girl and the desire for power of a man they did not even know, who did not even honour them with his hatred. And then, further still, almost imperceptible but present all the same, that young man who had gone missing, striding across a ghostly empire, staggering through the garbage among the zebus and the whores, who had resigned

181

himself to living in the wrong century, he would stop dreaming of shakos, gilded anchors on uniform sleeves, opium dens and royalty, he did not want the redemption of the world, but would settle for life, and now, unrecognisable, he found himself many years later all but dead, yet designated to redeem the world. Vincent wiped his eyes. He oiled and assembled his hunting rifle that had been sleeping in his closet for years. He went and got the twelve-calibre bullets. With a knife, he dug deep grooves into them in the form of a cross so they would fragment at the moment of impact. He loaded the rifle and put it back in the closet. He looked at himself in the mirror. He looked like death, even more so, perhaps, than usual. Strange. His lost soul was beckoning him, life was returning. But the only thing he felt was pain and terrible exhaustion He went to the bar.

He talked with Théodore Moracchini. He told him about the eyes of the zebu. He was full of nostalgia. He would have been better off staying there, and too bad for redemption. Back there, many things inspired anguish. He was too young, he did not know that anguish is a sign of vitality. Since returning, anguish had deserted him. There had been enthusiasm, then nothing. Théodore listened to him benevolently, then left. Vincent watched Hayet. Just then, Virginie, full of happiness, came into the bar. She stood in front of Vincent.

"He's coming tonight, you'll see. He just called me."

"Tonight?" Vincent repeated.

She smiled. It was not happiness after all, it was a challenge, like the evening before.

"Yes. Tonight," she confirmed. "I told you. No-one can keep him from coming to see me. No-one."

She left the bar.

"Hayet?" Vincent called.

"Yes?" she said, a little surprised that Vincent had something to say to her.

"I have to go home."

"Yes?" she repeated, as if to ask him what he was getting at.

Vincent lowered his eyes. He sighed.

"But I'll be back tomorrow," he said finally.

"Alright."

When she saw her daughter rush upstairs to her room and lock the door, Marie-Angèle understood that Stéphane would be visiting. She would not be able to sleep and would have to spend the evening reading with earplugs in her ears. She could always spend the night with Théodore Moracchini, but even though she knew Virginie was insensible to her blame and disapproval, she did not want her daughter thinking she was giving her free rein. It was a question of dignity. She would not be put out of her own house.

Upstairs, Virginie was triumphant, as she was each time she knew Stéphane was coming, but her heart was gripped by the shadow of a horrible premonition that hovered over her. To escape the feeling, she took a long, perfumed bath, soaking with devotion, trying to turn her mind to happy thoughts. Then she carefully softened her skin, massaging it with a moisturising cream that smelled of vanilla and patchouli. After completely shaving between her legs, she sat cross-legged in front of her mirror, armed with tweezers, and began minutely hunting down any hairs she might have missed. When she finished, it was still early. She slipped on a pair of socks and placed the black silk blindfold over her eyes. Two hours ahead of time, she lay down, completely sightless, and pressed her feet against the far side of each bedpost. In the darkness she tried to think of Stéphane, then concentrated on the cramps in her adductors so the discomfort would absorb her entirely, but she could not avoid the certainty that something terrible was about to happen. The more she tried to push away that feeling, the harder her heart beat. She did not feel the cramp anymore, nor the irritation of her sensitive skin. She heard only her heart and then, later, after night fell, a car engine, and a gunshot, like the terrible beating of a second exploding heart, and she screamed, there was a second gunshot, she knew something terrible really had happened, and what that thing was. She ripped off her blindfold and ran down the stairs, howling.

The sun was about to set and the air had cooled. The car windows were down and Stéphane's migraine was fading. The closer he drew to Virginie's village, the more he wanted to accelerate. It was something he could not control. Images of tender, hairless skin tormented him, memories of biting into a fleshy mound, moist secretions and the penetration of teeth. In the midst of those things was the inalterable, celestial feeling that he was loved more than any other human being had been loved in this world. Maybe that was why he could not pull away from Virginie. A love that reached from the abyss to the vault of the skies, demanding a new language, or speaking the barbarous tongue of the absolute in which truth and lie are indiscernible. Stéphane was proud. He was what he had wanted to be. He had discovered how to use all the resources of forgetting the way conquering souls do. The memory of the victors is selective, he had always known that. When it does not completely erase undesirable memories, it knows how to shroud them in mist; that is the mark of its strength. A quiet mist covered three bloody corpses, anonymous, feature-less. The victorious soul knows how to coexist with the depths of the abyss and the heights of heaven. It does not give in to the weight of its acts the way Tony succumbed to the weight of an action too great for him. Stéphane did not stare into the darkness with the fear that a ghost might appear from it or, worse, that no ghost would ever step forward. The victorious soul does not fear solitude, it reigns alone over the present, its creation, it inhabits it wholly and nothing drags it backwards. No animal stare. No lost youth. No luminous promenade overlooking the

Atlantic that no-one will ever walk again. Stéphane brought no judgment to bear on what he had done. The things of the past find their justification in the present, and there is nothing more to say about them. It is pointless returning to them. The migraine had disappeared, Stéphane stopped thinking about it, he savoured the unspeakable pleasure of relief. The night air filled his lungs, the stink lingered but he stopped smelling it. Up ahead, he saw light flowing from Virginie's window and he accelerated because he knew she was waiting for him with her love – the highest love in the world, the deepest, love that had no end.

Vincent patted the barrel of his gun. He was cold. He thought of summer nights marked by the plaintive hooting of an owl. The owl would have helped him pass the time. He was neither moved nor afraid. He waited, sitting behind a wall, watching Virginie's glowing window. The growl of the motor was so distant at first he thought the noise was coming from inside his head. Then the sound grew closer. The car was moving fast. It pulled up near him. He heard the gravel flying beneath the tyres and the brakes squealing. The motor stopped. When he heard the door slam, he stood up. Stéphane was a few metres away, his back turned. When Vincent drew near, he turned around. He must have seen the weapon, yet he waved and smiled. That must have been an automatic reaction, the kind you make when you recognise someone and you're too absorbed by other things to remember you haven't spoken to that person in years. Vincent pointed the barrel towards Stéphane's stomach. As he did it, he thought he should remember Dominique and Hayet too, but he couldn't think of anything other than pointing his weapon in the right direction. Stéphane was still smiling. Vincent wondered briefly if he should say something, to be sure Stéphane understood what was happening, and why, and he was still wondering when he heard the gun go off, and right away, afterwards, Virginie screaming from inside the house. He must have pulled the trigger. Stéphane was lying on the gravel. Vincent moved closer and leaned over him. There was no use talking now, and, anyway, he had nothing to say. When he fired the second shot into his guts at point-blank range, he smelled the stink of shit. He turned around and went home the long way, trying to get the smell out of his nostrils. Virginie was still screaming. Vincent did not run, there was no reason to, he walked calmly along the path, no hurry, but his heart was beating as hard as if he had run the whole way.

Back home, he broke down the weapon, cleaned it and oiled it. He made something to eat and watched a little television. Then he went and sat down on the edge of the bed. He looked at his hands. He awaited the return of his lost soul. He waited a long time. Only his heart was beating. Everyone was freed but him. In the calm of the night, Marie-Angèle fell asleep, comforted by Théodore Moracchini's shoulder. In her room, purified by misfortune and tears, Virginie fell sleep too, dreaming of the majesty of white queens in mourning. Shadows bowed respectfully before the sanctity of her grief as she walked on a bed of flowers, along the frozen path of eternal youth. Stéphane had entered the luminous garden of martyrs for whom incense celebrated the crowning of a perfect life. Far below him lay the dealers and the traitors, in the shadows with neither glory nor name. Vincent lay down on his bed and turned off the light. He did not sleep. The darkness was empty. He thought, in her room above the bar, that Hayet was not sleeping either. She was there, so near, they were the only ones keeping watch in the serenity of a sleeping world, eyes wide open on the depths of the night, where he could never reach her, for they drifted side by side in their loneliness, behind barriers of nostalgia, without even a spirit to console them.

A New Library from MacLehose Press

This book is part of a new international library for literature in translation. MacLehose Press has become known for its wide-ranging list of best-selling European crime writers, eclectic non-fiction and winners of the Nobel and Independent Foreign Fiction prizes, and for the many awards given to our translators. In their own countries, our writers are celebrated as the very best.

Join us on our journey to **READ THE WORLD**.

www.maclehosepress.com